Guardians for the Vamp

Settle Myer

Contents

A Note from the Author

Guardians for the Vamp is a FFM fated mates romance. The characters fall fast & hard. This book is a standalone featuring Layla & Vara from A Vow for the Vamp & Thorne from Gaga for the Gargoyle.

This book contains explicit content and some difficult topics. There will be A LOT of graphic sex between ALL my characters. Like... they're all horny. This book has plot but the sex outweighs plot. If that's not for you, you probably won't like this book.

There will also be blood play, voyeurism, exhibitionism, butt stuff (with tails and magical peens), drugs/drug use, death, violence, kidnapping, discussions of domestic abuse (mental, physical, verbal), discussions of abuse of a minor, discussions of infertility, discussions of an arranged marriage of a minor, and death of loved ones (off page). If you have concerns, or a specific trigger, please reach out to the author.

====================

Please note that while I have named real NYC locations in this book, I've also added some fake locations/businesses.

======================

Let's talk about anal. This book is not a manual. If you're going to do butt stuff, please research to avoid injury. PLEASE PREPARE. My characters are MONSTERS with supernatural healing so I didn't include much prep work for them. Do not do what they do!

Help is available

Suicide & Crisis Lifeline — Call or Text: 988

https://988lifeline.org/

https://afsp.org/

https://nami.org/Home

National Domestic Violence Hotline: 800-799-7233 or

Text START to 88788

https://www.thehotline.org/

Please consider donating to St. Jude:

https://www.stjude.org/

Playlist

Wonderful Tonight – Eric Clapton

Don't Threaten Me With A Good Time – Panic! At the Disco

Scars – I Prevail

When A Man Loves A Woman – Percy Sledge

Your Guardian Angel – The Red Jumpsuit Apparatus

Nothing's Gonna Stop Us Now – Starship

Can't Fight This Feeling – REO Speedwagon

Truly Madly Deeply – Savage Garden

Broken – Seether, Amy Lee

Kiss From A Rose – Seal

Dedication

This is for the readers who always wanted to be double stuffed by two monster tails.

Chapter 1 - Layla

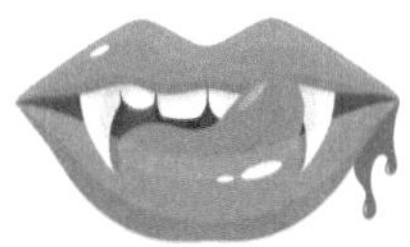

I'm nervous as fuck.

I'm never nervous.

I hate the feeling of my stomach twisting and my nerves vibrating like a live wire.

If I had a heartbeat, I'd surely be dead from a heart attack.

I wasn't even this nervous when I was crowned vampire queen of New York City just over three months ago.

It's the highest honor for my kind. Well, in title only, I suppose. There are elders far more important than me; vampires who have reached four digits in age—like the first vampire who is so old, it's rumored he rarely requires blood to survive. It's been centuries since he's made any sort of public appearance, only glimpses of the broody man lingering in the shadows.

My little promotion is nothing compared to those vampires, but that still doesn't negate the fact that I, Layla Sofia Aldana, was chosen for this role.

I remember walking into the World Organization of Vampire Elites—WOVE—headquarters in Lower Manhattan for my coronation with my head held high. I was asked to arrive early so the Council of Vampire Elites or COVE—WOVE's governing body—could inform me of unprecedented changes happening during my reign, including having a gargoyle head my security team that will be comprised of a variety of supernatural beings.

It's not common for high-ranking supernaturals to have different species on their protection detail. In fact, I only know of one: my best friend Millie, and the former vampire queen, who has two griffin guards.

Even more unprecedented is asking a *gargoyle* to protect another supernatural being. Gargoyles protect cities, towns, and small villages. They're destined to protect innocent human souls, not vampire queens. They only assist us when a vampire goes mad with blood lust and threatens the lives of humans.

So why?

The elder vampires, and other supernatural leaders, are tired of living in the shadows. They want to reveal our world to the humans, but in order to do that, we all have to be on the same page. That begins with unification, working together in all aspects of our lives.

They're testing this unification plan with me.

Tonight I've been tasked with asking King Basque if he'd lend me one of his soldiers. COVE was supposed to speak with the gargoyle king three months ago, but he's canceled all scheduled meetings with them up until now. Understandable since he's been dealing with the aftermath of his brother, Magnus, trying to steal his throne.

Magnus wanted to reign over New York City and cause harm, or death, to humans. It was eerily similar to the failed attempt by feral vampire Heinrich—Millie's sire—who wanted to form an army of supernaturals and capture humans to farm them for blood.

Thankfully, both of those fuckers are now dead.

I'm not surprised COVE wants me to be the one to break the news to the gargoyle king. They know I won't complain. They know I won't try to back out. Because they know how badly I want to lead.

The role of vampire queen doesn't typically involve much responsibility, mostly acting as a mediator or over-seeing policy creations, even though new policies for vampires haven't been constructed in decades. The queen can also decide the fate of a rogue vampire. Depending on their crimes, she can choose death by sun or stake to the heart or an eternity in a cell.

Millie hated being queen. She only agreed to the job because it was during a time when vampires needed rules. I became her royal advisor about one hundred years ago, offering her any support she needed. She claims I was the one in charge, but she's wrong. She was a great ruler.

She left the role—naming me as her successor—after meeting her blood mate: A golden retriever man destined to a lifetime of love with a creature of the night. Blood mates are rare for vampires. We're cursed beings not meant for love. We claim. *Possess.* We have no souls.

Yet my bestie found her soulmate.

Bonding with Teddy physically changed her. The sun's rays can no longer kill her—though if she spends too much time in the sun, it will make her sick. Her heart also beats, even if those beats are slower than normal. Her tears no longer bleed.

I was overjoyed for her, but I couldn't deny my jealousy. A vampire in love? It proves that we're capable of the emotion... that maybe the curse upon our kind is wrong, and we're not soulless evil abominations.

It doesn't matter. The chances of me finding my blood mate, when Millie is only the third vampire to do so, are low. I'm 709 years old, and I've long accepted I will be alone forever.

Not that I have time for love... or to even fool around anymore.

A week after my coronation, COVE informed me that I'll be leading a special committee comprised of representatives from every supernatural species living in New York City. Our sole purpose will be forming a plan to reveal ourselves to humans.

We have to prepare for the unknown, the council had told me. *Humans are extremely emotional. There could be an uprising. The ones who hunt us, and other supernatural beings, could form an army. The human government could capture us to experiment. If that happens, the supes will retaliate, especially if it threatens their lives or that of their mates.*

The heavy wooden doors to the grand hall open, pulling me from my thoughts.

"Lala!" a familiar voice calls out.

Teddy's nickname for me is new, and I don't hate it. My name isn't one that can easily transform into something cute... like Milli Vanilli, which is what Teddy calls his mate.

I brace myself for an onslaught of energy from the former human who was turned into a vampire not too long ago.

Within seconds, he crosses the hardwood floor to reach me where I stand near the back of the room. He lets out a 'woo!' and a smile stretches over his face.

"That never gets old."

He's clearly enjoying his new vampire abilities.

Millie walks through the entrance at normal speed. She dodges vampire workers speeding around, making final preparations for tonight's party, including hanging decorations and setting out drinks and food—all tailored to tonight's guests: blood for vampires, fairie wine for the fae, human food for shifters, weres, and witches.

"I need a leash," Millie mumbles.

"Yes!" Teddy says, wiggling his eyebrows at my friend.

Millie's fangs drop, and I imagine the image of Teddy wearing a leash while crawling to her just popped into her head, because it unfortunately popped into my head too.

"Lala," Teddy gasps. "Stop thinking about me naked on all fours being led around by a leash."

Fucker.

"You got me." I sigh, but it's hard not to smile at the disgustingly positive man. I'm a positive person too, but Teddy's level of happiness is as if his endorphins are infused with crack.

Millie smiles at our bickering and it's so foreign on her. She used to be a grump but now she radiates joy. Teddy has clearly infected her with his sunshine personality.

And I absolutely love that for her.

"You look stunning," I say to my best friend.

I admire her glittering red gown that hugs her thick body and has sleeves that hang off her shoulders.

Millie and I are what the world considers plus-size. My stomach jiggles, and my thighs have dimples. I've lived in this bigger body for hundreds of years, but it was never seen as a problem—at least, not like it has in this modern society, which is obsessed with body image.

"Me? What about you? You're absolutely glowing."

I huff out a laugh. "Vampires do not glow... or sparkle for that matter."

Millie reaches up and adjusts my crown. It has purple jewels that were ethically mined in Australia and comes with a costly price tag. I explained to COVE that I didn't need a purple jeweled crown, but it arrived a few days after I'd been asked my favorite color.

The head piece is just a formality. Rarely worn unless there's an event, like the ball taking place tonight, where everyone goes overboard with extravagant outfits and headwear.

Millie's silver and black eyes water as she takes me in. I haven't seen her since my coronation. She avoids functions attended by a large number of supernaturals because Teddy's blood, being Millie's blood mate, is highly desirable to other supes. We still have no idea exactly why his blood is so special. We assume it has something to do with whatever magical property deemed the former human destined to be Millie's mate. Whatever the reason, Millie is highly protective of him and to lessen his appeal, she had a witch cast a protection spell over him.

"You make such a beautiful queen," Millie says, her voice catching. Being the strong-willed woman she is, she's quick to replace the emotion. Another smile spreads across her pale face. "We just ran into the gargoyles in the hallway. Who do you think will be your new head of security? Locheran maybe?"

"Who cares? They're all fucking hot," Teddy adds.

Millie bites her lip, nodding her agreement.

"I'll gladly let any of them ruin me," Teddy continues. His face lights up, and he grabs Millie's face, smooshing her cheeks. "Babe, we should ask the one with the scar if he wants to be our third." Teddy turns to me. "Not permanently. Just for funsies. And let me tell you, LaLa, the gargoyle is big—"

"All gargoyles are big," I mumble, but that doesn't stop Teddy from talking.

"—and, like, godly hot. First time meeting a gargoyle, and I'm in love." His eyes widen, and he wraps his arm around Millie's shoulders. "Not real love, that's only for my Milli Vanilli."

He kisses her temple.

"Yeah, I'm going to need you to calm down, puppy," I say, calling him by *his* nickname. "And, no, I don't know which one it will be because the king doesn't know about this request."

"Still?" Millie gasps.

"Yeah. COVE gave up after King Basque kept canceling meetings with them, so they informed me it's now my job as vampire queen to hold meetings with other supernatural royals."

"Definitely pick the beefy one," Teddy says, not even focusing on the other part of our conversation.

He runs his fingers through his shaggy blond hair, then unbuttons his suit jacket to reveal his dress shirt stretched over his gut. Teddy has a dad bod—another descriptor the body-image obsessed world has adopted for men who don't have abs.

"I have to say," Millie begins, raising a brow at me twirling a wayward curl at the nape of my neck. "I've never seen you anxious before. Not even at your coronation. I mean, you freaked out for a second, but the moment you took the stage, that strong woman I love took over. Are you nervous about the unification plan?"

I drop the curl and shift on my feet. "Yes. It's going to be a disaster. You know how supernaturals are. We're stubborn, and we don't like being told what to do. It's not going to work."

"Do you know how long they've been considering this plan to reveal ourselves to the human world? I'm a little offended they didn't include me in discussions."

"Miss 'I want to face the sun because I hate my life', of course they didn't get you involved. But apparently it's been in discussions for months. And since you've been wanting to step away from the throne for years, they need-ed someone more... reliable to launch the plan."

She rolls her eyes, and I stifle the urge to choke my best friend. The night she met her mate, she had planned to end her existence. Millie's sire forced her to do some really fucked up shit after he turned her into a vampire, and she was tired of living with her guilt.

Teddy saved her life.

I was pissed when she told me she wanted to face the sun. She never talked to me about having these feelings. I could have been there for her. *I* could have been the one to save her, but she shut me out, as most vampires do with emotions.

The doors open again, and we turn as three tall and massive gargoyles enter.

I've met the king and the commander of his army, Locheran, plenty of times before. But this third gargoyle...

Holy shit he's intimidating.

The scar that got Teddy and Millie all hot and bothered stretches diagonally across his dark purple face. Braided black hair hangs over his shoulder. His light purple wings are tucked to his back, and his tail whips around his body as if agitated.

My eyes lift up and up, past his pointed ears, until finding dark gray horns that curve out of each side of his forehead. Lord, he's tall. I'm five foot four and this gargoyle is as tall as the king, who I'm pretty sure is seven feet. Xander and Locheran are both packed with muscles, but this soldier? He's bulkier. Thicker. A mountain of a monster.

My amplified vampire senses pick up a new scent, one not belonging to Xander or Locheran. Sandalwood—my *favorite*—and hints of cinnamon wash over me.

Fuck... this new gargoyle smells fantastic.

His plump lips purse as they stop a foot in front of us.

What the hell? Is he mad about being here? Why so grumpy?

"Queen Aldana," Xander says, pulling my attention away from the Goliath of a gargoyle. The king holds out a hand, and I place mine in his, giving it a firm shake before letting it go and stepping back in line with the other two.

"Lovely to see you again, King Basque," I peer over his shoulder. "I was hoping to meet your mate. Is she not attending tonight's ball?"

Xander and his mate skipped my coronation, sending Locheran in his place following the fallout of his brother's attempted coup. I assume he didn't want his mate to attend without him by her side.

It's clear the gargoyle king is madly in love, his face lights up at the thought of the human. "Since you asked that I arrive early, Evangeline will be arriving separately with her mother."

I nod and make a note to find them at the party so I can meet the human who saved the gargoyle king of New York City. Gargoyles in royal positions are cursed to find their mate by their thousandth year of living or permanently turn to stone. Xander had six months left to live before he found Evangeline.

Talk about a close call.

I glance at tall, dark, and handsome again, but he's scanning the room instead of paying me any attention. As if he's looking for a way to escape. Or maybe he's scoping out potential threats as gargoyles tend to do, their protective nature kicking in no matter where they are. Either way, he's yet to look at me, which for some reason pisses me off. Who the hell is this guy anyway?

Okay, wow, I'm being needy. He does *not* owe me his attention.

"Congratulations on your new position," Xander says. "I'm sorry I couldn't attend your crowning ceremony, but I'm here now. Please tell the elder vamps to stop blowing up my inbox and text messages."

The king chuckles, and my anxiety lessens slightly. Xander has always been a reasonable leader, but there's no telling how he'll react to this request to have one of his soldiers lead my security team.

I wonder which one it will be.

Xander waves a hand to Locheran. "Of course, you know the commander of my army."

Locheran smiles, flashing me his fangs as he gives me a two fingered salute.

Xander motions to the broody gargoyle on his right who continues to act strangely. Apparently, the floor is the most interesting thing in the room.

"And this is Thorne."

Thorne.

Thorne.

I swear my heart flutters at the name, which is impossible because I'm dead and my heart no longer beats.

Thorne looks up at me—*finally*—and the fluttering moves lower.

Okay, Thorne can*not* lead my security team. I'm way too attracted to this massive gargoyle.

Chapter 2 - Thorne

My eyes fall to the new vampire queen just in time to notice a flash of what appears to be annoyance, possibly disdain, cross her face.

What the hell?

We've never met, yet she's already annoyed with me?

Or maybe she's repulsed by what she sees.

I mean, sure, I don't talk much—especially compared to loudmouth Locheran—and I'm not as handsome as him and Xander. I've got battle scars all over my body. The most prominent one across my face. I don't miss the way others cower, their eyes widening when I approach with my rugged and massive body.

I'm intimidating, sure, but sometimes I don't want to be.

Sometimes I just want to cuddle on a couch with someone and watch a romantic comedy and cry when the couple reunites at the end.

Sometimes I just want to be the little spoon for once.

Sometimes I just want to be told to get on my knees and beg my lover to punish me.

Whoa... where did that thought come from?

I haven't had thoughts like that in... decades. Thoughts that began the moment we walked in, and I saw *her*. My cock jerked with need. I didn't know how to act so my eyes nervously scanned the room, looking anywhere but at her.

I've been alive for 712 years. I've had partners of all genders and species, but sex became boring to me. I stopped feeling attraction. Even when Locheran drags me to nightclubs and drunk beings rub up against us, my body just doesn't respond.

But now. *Now,* as I take in Layla's light brown skin, her dark brown eyes, her mahogany hair that falls in elegant and loose curls around her head, her small breasts and soft body underneath the stretched fabric of her violet dress... my heart flutters, my stomach twists, and my cock hardens against my black cargo pants.

A throat clears and Locheran punches me in the shoulder, reaching around Xander to do so.

I snap out of it and notice Layla holding out her hand.

"It's nice to meet you, Thorne. I look forward to working with you," she says.

I move to take her greeting. Wait, maybe I shouldn't touch her. If I'm feeling this way from just a glance at her voluptuous body, then skin-to-skin contact will surely cause me to combust.

I drop my hand. She frowns and pulls her hand back, but I'm already extending mine out again. Her brows furrow, and she doesn't move to accept my confused greeting so I lower my hand, which of course, is when she decides to reach out hers out one final time.

"Are you well?" she asks, balling her hand into a fist and dropping it to her side.

No. I'm not well. I am literally dying inside.

Words, Thorne! Use them!

But I can't so I answer the vampire with a nod. I'm... flustered, and I don't understand why.

"Do you not... speak?"

Humor fills Layla's voice as she regards Locheran and Xander who stare at me like I've grown an extra tail and a horn out of my ass.

Xander slaps his palm on my shoulder not-so-gently.

"He's a gargoyle of few words."

Great. He's probably pissed. Or at least disappointed. I'm sure I've embarrassed him.

Layla purses her lips and glances at her friends, the former vampire queen Millie and her fledgling. The two are huddled together, palms over their mouths, clearly amused by what can only be explained as madness on my part.

"Okay then," Layla says. Her smooth honey voice washes over me like a warm shower on a cold winter night. "The attendees will be arriving shortly for the ball. Shall we head to the war room to meet?"

"Lead the way," Xander says.

Layla says goodbye to Millie and the blond man, telling them she'll see them later at the party. Once she turns to leave, Locheran nudges me with his elbow.

"Hey, so you were super weird just now."

"Was I?" I elbow him back.

"You definitely were," Xander says, furrowing his brows.

He's probably regretting bringing me to this meeting. The vampire queen asked Xander to bring a few of his top soldiers. We're not sure what she could possibly need help with, perhaps wrangling another rogue vampire, but it doesn't matter. I was honored Xander chose me.

I've been beating myself up over the past three months after Xander's brother betrayed him. His sister betrayed him, too, and I failed to notice. Elara was my partner on patrols more times than not. How did I not know she was being manipulated by Magnus and forced to help him? If only I had caught on sooner...

I scrub a palm over my face and straighten my posture. That's all water under the bridge. Xander made it clear that Elara had tricked everyone. He does not fault me.

"You're right. I *was* weird. I just... wasn't sure how to greet her."

"If you say so, buddy," Locheran snorts.

They know that's not the reason. They know I've greeted many kings and queens in my lifetime. I simply can't explain what's happening. It's as if my body is vibrating with... anxiety? Lust? Both?

I ignore Locheran and enter the war room behind him. Layla sits at the front of the table with a few of her bodyguards standing behind her against the wall. Xander takes a seat next to the vampire queen with Locheran on her other side. Layla inspects her manicured nails, as if doing whatever necessary to avoid eye contact with me, as I take my seat next to Locheran.

She clears her throat.

"Thank you for meeting with me before tonight's celebration," she begins.

There's a slight quaver in her voice. She's nervous. I fight the urge to stand and go to her... to hold her in my arms and ease whatever is causing this anxiety.

"I was informed a few weeks ago by the Council of Vampire Elites that they have been in discussions with other supernatural leaders about... um... revealing ourselves to the humans."

Locheran leans in and Xander's mouth drops open, but he snaps it shut, letting her continue.

"Right, I had the same reaction. It's something that would need in-depth planning, which is why COVE wants to form a committee with representatives from all supernatural communities so we can work out the details of how to make this happen as smoothly as possible. I'm to meet with leaders this week to discuss their recommendations for that committee. COVE would also like for my security team to be somewhat of a test of this unification plan."

Layla purses her lips and scrunches her nose like an adorable bunny. An adorable, but uncertain, bunny. Her hesitation tugs at my heart.

Layla's eyes snap to me.

Shit.

I place my hand over my chest as if that will stop the traitorous organ from beating so fast.

Can she hear me pining for her? Of course she can. She's a vampire. Her hearing is even better than my own supernatural hearing.

Layla's eyes hesitantly slide back to Xander. "King Basque... would you be interested in a partnership? One that involves having a gargoyle head my security team?"

The room is painfully silent for a few seconds, and I'm pretty sure the drumming of my frantic heartbeat has gotten louder.

Choose me. I would love to protect you.

I want to scream it out and claim this woman to be mine. If that means being her head of security, then I'll gladly accept the role. Yet I don't want to appear eager, especially after acting so strangely earlier.

Xander takes a sip from the glass of water in front of him and clears his throat.

"That's... quite the request, Queen Aldana."

She sighs. "Yes, and I understand if it's one you would not be interested in fulfilling. However, it's the 21st century. It's time we finally stop hiding. The humans are ready, especially with all the television shows, movies, and books about us. But in order for them to accept our existence, we supernaturals have to show a united front. We can't convince the humans we're of no threat to them—no more of a threat than their fellow humans—unless we ourselves are amicable."

It makes sense.

I've always wondered what it would be like to have humans know about our existence. There are a few who already know, who work with us during the day when the sun turns us to stone, but to convince an entire population that we aren't here to cause them harm?

It could end up being a disaster.

"Why a gargoyle?" Xander asks.

My stomach drops. Is he going to say no? Despite how badly I want to protect this woman, I couldn't defy my king and accept the role.

Even if I *beg* for the role.

Layla shrugs. "I wasn't given a reason, but I will say there's no better choice. Gargoyles are why this city still exists. You are loyal guardians, fierce warriors, strong and intelligent, and I'd be honored to have one of your soldiers by my side, especially with all the unknowns that come with this unveiling plan."

My chest puffs with pride. Locheran and Xander sit taller.

"After these two most recent incidents with Heinrich and your brother," Layla continues, her voice softening. She's beautiful *and* compassionate. "The vampire elders and other supernatural leaders want to avoid another power-hungry monster from trying to take over the human world. We want to reveal ourselves peacefully, not forcefully. Elder supes have been discussing this for months. Did you not get the invitation to those meetings?"

Xander winces. "I was invited but being that I was months away from permanently turning to stone, I declined to get involved in any supernatural related business."

My heart hurts for my king. He had begun to lose hope before his fated mate entered his life.

"When must I decide?" Xander asks.

Layla grimaces.

"Now? They want to present my new head of security at tonight's ball."

I swallow to wet my dry throat, not loving the idea of her working the crowd.

She's the host. She'll be networking, shaking hands with other supernatural leaders. There will be dancing and flirting and food—for the supes who can eat—and booze or intoxicated human donors for supes who can only get high off drunk or drugged blood.

I've been to enough supernatural parties to know that they evolve into heavy touching, middle-of-the-dance-floor make out sessions, and full-on sex on the stage for an audience of voyeurs.

Yet the thought of someone else touching Layla, let alone kissing or fucking her, makes my blood boil.

All heads turn to me. I lock eyes with Layla for a few seconds—her pupils expanding to black orbs—before she covers her mouth and looks away.

Did I see her fangs drop?

"You growled, bro," Locheran says out of the corner of his mouth. "You look like you want to murder someone."

Fuck.

I'm losing my mind. That's got to be the only explanation. I'm never so... passionate... about anything, let alone any*one*. I learned a long time ago that feelings only lead to heartbreak.

"It's unprecedented," Xander grumbles, ignoring my wayward emotions. "But I don't want to be uncooperative either."

Xander twists the small glass of water in his large hands then sighs.

"Very well. I'll provide you with a soldier for a month as a test run. If it doesn't work out, you'll need to find another supernatural to assume the role."

Layla nods. "And who do you... suggest?"

She bites her lip, glancing down at her hands crossed regally on the tabletop.

"I can't lend you Locheran. He leads my army, and if you need a representative for the committee you mentioned, then he'd be the one I'd recommend."

My chest tightens. He's going to say my name. This is it. I'm dying of a heart attack. My head throbs with how much adrenaline is rushing through my body.

"Thorne is my finest soldier. If he agrees, then he's yours."

"Mine?" Layla asks, her voice a pitch higher.

"Yes, your new head of security." Xander turns to me, an eyebrow raised in question.

I nod, words still failing me. Xander shakes his head, confused at my behavior. I may not speak a lot, but I *do* speak. Especially when my king is addressing me.

Layla lifts her head, her brown eyes briefly passing to me before she looks back at Xander, pursing her lips.

"Well? Does the silent one accept?"

A bark of laughter bursts out of Locheran. He attempts to cover it with a cough, which he chases down with a glass of water.

"He accepts," Xander answers.

"Okay," she says and stands. "Great."

Okay?

Great?

That's all she has to say?

You're one to talk. You've yet to say a word to the enchanting woman.

She extends her hand to Xander. "Thank you for your time. You're welcome to stay and socialize in here or head to the great hall for the party." Layla nods to me. "Thorne, if you could stay back so we can discuss some logistics."

I stifle a groan at my name on her lips.

I leave Xander and Locheran and walk to her side. She smells like flowers and the forest with hints of citrus and my heart kicks in my chest in response.

My cock also takes notice and twitches.

"I know this is all happening so fast, I do apologize," she begins, her eyes finding mine. A strange sensation flutters through my stomach... like butterflies flapping their wings, trying to escape. Wait. *Butterflies?* I can't remember the last time someone made me feel like a prepubescent pup with a crush. "As I mentioned, the president of the council for the World Organization of Vampire Elites will be introducing you as my new head of security tonight, and tomorrow you'll be expected to get right to work. I hope that's not a problem."

I shake my head, and she scrunches her nose—she's done that twice now, and I find it just as adorable as the first time—and hands me a folder that was sitting on the table in front of her.

"This packet has everything you'll need to know about my building's security measures as well as key cards to give you access to the elevator and my penthouse. As for security at tonight's party, everything's already planned. There will be plenty of guards in place throughout the ballroom. Your job tonight is to stand your handsome self next to me on stage, then we'll go around the room while I shake hands and pretend to smile at the important supes."

Her phone buzzes, and she picks it up, frustratingly typing out a text message.

"You think I'm handsome?"

She startles at my deep voice, her phone flipping out of her hands, but her quick vampire reflexes catch it before it hits the table. A smile tugs at my lips.

"Goddamn it, Thorne. Warn a girl the next time you're going to ear fuck me with that sexy velvety baritone."

She goes on mumbling something about narrating spicy audiobooks, and I don't ask how I could have warned her without speaking first. I also don't point out that she called me—well, my voice—sexy after just saying I'm handsome.

"Yeah, um, so, tomorrow we should meet to discuss my protection detail. Right now, my guards are solely vampires, but COVE would like me to hire other supernaturals to join my security team."

"Really?"

Supernatural beings are selfish. We don't work well with each other. I mean, we fuck each other sometimes, but actually being civil with each other? Most would never voluntarily work on another supe's security team. The former vampire queen is the only one that I know of with two griffin bodyguards.

"Yep." She pops the 'p.' "It's part of this unification plan, apparently. Remember I mentioned being amicable?"

I nod.

"That includes working together... becoming allies."

She blows a piece of hair that's fallen in her face, and I almost reach up to tuck it behind her ear.

Almost.

"So, tomorrow we'll go over profiles of candidates I was sent. You'd know more about their credentials than I would. We also need to decide which of the vampires currently on my team you'd like to keep. I have twenty guards now, at least five of those are humans who patrol my building during the day when I'm at rest."

I silently curse. She needs better daytime protection. Humans are no match for a supe who wants to harm Layla when she's most vulnerable. I'm going to double her detail. She'll need supes who can withstand the sun keeping guard.

I'm already eager to go through profiles with her, even though the thought of being alone with her makes my stupid heart race again. I can't explain it. All I know is I keep thinking about all the dirty things I want to do to this woman if I had her alone. Things I shouldn't be thinking of as her new head of security.

"I hope I didn't offend you," I say.

She raises a brow. "Wow, you've now spoken two coherent sentences. Congratulations."

I ignore the sass and continue.

"I seem to have annoyed you somehow. If it was the greeting, I apologize—"

"It wasn't," she interrupts, her eyes down and refusing to look at me again. "I'm sorry, I'm just..."

I lift my hand to clutch her chin but stop, remembering I have no right to comfort her... to touch her.

I'm *dying* to touch her.

It's as if her beauty... her defiance and power... is awakening my body from a decades-old slumber. I inhale deeply, attempting to calm myself down but instead, Layla's scent overwhelms me. Not just her perfume... but her cunt.

Her *wet* cunt.

Is that for me? Her pleasure? Is she dripping with want for me?

Layla stiffens beside me, and I realize I growled—*again*—the sound rumbling deep in my chest. It would have been too low for a human across the room to hear it but, of course, everyone in the room is a supernatural being who are all now staring at the vampire queen and her new gargoyle guard.

How many times have I growled now for no reason?

She is the reason.

The door to the room opens, thankfully diverting our attention. Layla gasps, and I follow her eyes to the golden creature who just entered.

Vara.

The sphinx owns most of the supernatural nightclubs around New York City. We've never met, but I've heard plenty about her.

She walks in on all fours, like she's an A-list celebrity at a Hollywood movie premiere. Her wings stretch out as she scans the room, then as she stands on two feet, she shutters them to her back. Strutting towards us, her golden cat-like eyes lock on Layla and a tinge of jealousy and protectiveness nips at my nerves.

Vara glances at me and raises her brow. The corner of her lip turns up into a smirk, showing me a fang.

The curls of golden blonde hair fall around her like a mane. She's wearing a banded headpiece full of diamonds and other colorful jewels that I couldn't begin to name. The colors match her sparkling rainbow dress that looks more like lingerie and barely covers her furred body. Her lion's tail hangs beside her like a snake, ready to attack.

"My queen," she says to Layla the moment she stops in front of her. She bows for show.

Layla's brown eyes are wide, her pupils blown, plump lips parted. I spot the tips of her fangs. Is she... turned on by the sphinx?

The room has gone silent. Xander and Locheran move closer as if ready for the sphinx to attack. Not that Vara has a reputation of being violent, only that she's shown up to a meeting she wasn't invited to.

Vara tries to take Layla's hands into her paws, but before I can react, preparing to protect the vampire queen, Layla steps back.

"What are you doing here, Vara?" she asks, standing a little bit taller.

Vara glances at me again. Her eyes scan my body from head to toe before giving me a flirty wink, which sends a shiver rolling through my body.

What the hell?

Have I been poisoned by a succubus? An incubus? Or any other sexually charged demon? I've never been so hard in my life and the sexual tension between Vara and Layla isn't helping.

The two clearly have a history.

"I'm here for the party, of course."

Layla opens her mouth to speak but Vara cuts her off.

"And to let you know that I've been selected as the new ambassador to humans on the Supernatural Unveiling Committee."

"Excuse me?" Layla says.

Vara walks around Layla's left, her clawed hand dragging across the vampire queen's bare shoulder. I should step in, force the sphinx to stop touching the woman I'm now assigned to guard, but my cock grows harder as if sensing Layla's pleasure intensifying.

I can't move or everyone will see my tented pants.

"You see, my little Layla-lollipop, they're going to need a voice... a face for the public once we reveal ourselves to the humans."

"How do you know about the unveiling plan? I was given a list of every supe who was included in the discussions, and you weren't on it," Layla says, crossing her arms.

The move pushes her cleavage up, and I force myself to look away from the beautiful mounds.

"I have eyes and ears all over this city, my dear."

Vara stalks behind Layla, dragging her sharp fingertip across her back. Then she continues to me. Her palm flattens on my upper arm, and I nearly blow my load right then.

What the hell?

Vara grins at me like I'm a four-course meal she's about to devour and keeps walking until she's back in front of Layla. She cups the vamp's chin and leans in, their lips inches apart.

"You're stuck with me, my sweet Layla-cakes."

Vara is seconds from kissing Layla, but the vampire queen pulls back.

"You're crossing the line, *sphinx*," Layla warns, her fangs fully bared now.

The look on her face would frighten any human, maybe even a few young vampires and other supernatural beings.

Me?

I see desire and anger in a battle for dominance.

"*If* I get word that you formally have the position, then we will talk." Layla waves her hand, dismissing Vara. "Until then, you are not part of this meeting. That is all."

Fuck.

My cock leaks at the vampire's demanding words. I would love nothing more than to drop to my knees and beg her to smack me around.

Both women turn their heads to me, eyes wide, mouths open.

Okay. I clearly did something, but before either woman can question me, one of Layla's guards whisks Vara away and Xander takes Layla aside.

"Why are you all growly?" Locheran asks, clamping a hand on my shoulder.

Layla turns her head slightly while half paying attention to whatever Xander is going on about as if listening for my answer.

But I say nothing. Because I can't explain why I'm suddenly going feral for the new vampire queen... and strangely enough, the sphinx too.

Chapter 3 - Vara

Well, this is a surprise.

The moment I walked into the room, it was as if a force pulled me to the new vampire queen. I never expected that overwhelming need to include a gargoyle.

This is more than simple attraction.

I was drawn to Layla the first time we met when she'd accompanied a shifter to one of my clubs last year. She's lived in New York City for a century, yet our paths never crossed. Of course, I'd heard about her since she was the royal advisor for former vampire queen, Mildred Maycot. She was Millie's right-hand woman... her best friend. Layla was always by her side, so seeing her out and being social without Millie was surprising.

Layla was more beautiful than I could have imagined. The moment I took her hand in mine, I felt what can only be described as a current. Electricity lit up my entire body.

It was exciting but equally terrifying.

I've always been a loner. It's hard not to be when you're 2,000 years old, 2,056 to be exact. When I was younger and had family and friends—when I wasn't one of the last of my kind—I cared about conversations and being a part of another soul's life.

Then hunters murdered my parents and siblings for their golden feathers. I only survived because I was the youngest. The fastest. I escaped and hid for hundreds of years deep inside what is now called the Wadi Sannur Cave in Beni Suef, Egypt. When I emerged, sphinxes were merely a legend. My body evolved to survive, gaining the ability to mask so I can blend in with the human world.

I don't trust easily. Love comes even harder for me. I enjoy sex and physical touch but not the emotion that comes with it.

So I didn't immediately seek Layla out to explore this strange feeling. But over the past year, I couldn't get that night out of my head. I regret not at least speaking with her. I reached out to Millie a few months ago and begged her to bring her royal advisor to any of the clubs I owned. Millie refused.

I asked for Layla's number, or for Millie to give her mine... anything, but Millie said it wasn't up to her. Layla clearly didn't want to see me either or maybe what she felt between us also scared her. While I could have easily tracked Layla down, I wasn't going to push her to see me without her consent.

Shortly before Layla was crowned, I heard about the plan to reveal ourselves to humans and how they wanted her to lead the effort. Apparently, the elder councils for all supernatural beings have been discussing it for months. I was furious that I was never included. The elders have no idea what they're doing. Most of them are old-fashioned and refuse to adapt to the modern world. They needed me. I went to COVE and presented my case. I reminded them of my status amongst our kind and how I can sway any supernatural to my side. That's all it took for them to create the human ambassador role for me.

It's been a year since I last saw Layla and she's just as beautiful, just as fierce.

She *dismissed* me!

Rightfully so. I couldn't wait for the party so I crashed the meeting. A meeting I didn't know was taking place, only that my body knew where to go and led me to the war room.

She was surprised to see me... she was turned on... probably confused, too, which might be what angered her.

Now I'm being led away from her, and the gargoyle guard, feeling as if my heart is being ripped from my chest. That terrifying and electric connection I first experienced upon meeting Layla a year ago happened again the moment I put my hand on the massive, scarred monster whose name I still don't know.

I don't understand.

I need a moment to calm down—to think—and disappear into the bathroom. When I emerge fifteen minutes later and enter the grand hall, I glance around the room, searching for familiar faces. I spot Millie with her new mate, who is speaking animatedly with Xander, the gargoyle king. He listens intently to the hyper fledgling vampire.

Next to Xander is his new mate, a human named Evangeline. The short and thick woman laughs at whatever Locheran just said. She shakes her head and rolls her eyes. I immediately like her because exasperation is the only way to react to Locheran Perrier.

An older woman with gray hair stands beside Evangeline, and I sense her power from clear across the room. She's a witch but one I haven't met yet.

My eyes travel around the rest of the grand hall.

Malachi, the fae prince is here with his court.

Gregor, the werewolf alpha, stands at the back with his beta. They're speaking quietly while glaring at Philandria, alpha of the wolf shifters, who is here with two of her pack members. Wolf shifters are different from were-wolves, who require a full moon to shift while wolf shifters can turn at will. There are also other animal shifters like panthers and bears, though they aren't as prominent as the wolves.

Saoirse, witch and coven leader, stands off to the side with a small group of witches.

Aaron, a spirit, lingers in the shadows. He's the only one not dressed in his finest attire, since he died in the 90s wearing punk rocker clothes. Ghosts are tethered to the place they died, which might be the only reason he's here tonight. He has nothing better to do.

Wylan, tribe leader of the centaurs, is along the wall, arms crossed as if he's ready to fight.

Gorgan, the only dragon that I know of living on the East Coast, is in his human form and mimics the centaur's pose.

Hallerin, griffin prince, flirts with some of the women in Malachi's court—who are clearly ignoring him.

Lorian, a demon, sulks in a chair at a back wall clearly not wanting to be here. He must have been nominated to attend the party since there are no leaders amongst the demons. They're all degenerate cunts.

Not surprisingly, there are no angel representatives here because they're also degenerate cunts.

Despite the righteous angels, everyone who could physically be here is here. The entire supe community has been obsessed with Layla's succession. Her coronation was historic.

There are tens of thousands of supernaturals living in the Big Apple and each species has its own leader. Leadership that rarely changes power, like Xander who has reigned over the gargoyles, protecting New York City since it was merely a settlement called New Amsterdam. And Millie who reigned over New York City vampires since the mid-1800s.

That's why crowning a new vampire queen was exciting for our world. Being immortal means running out of new experiences. It means no longer finding joy in things, in everyday life, in companionship. It means skirting rules and morals just to get a spark of adrenaline. It's why vampires go mad with blood lust, or why the fae like to make sketchy deals with humans.

Owning supernatural nightclubs, I'm constantly around a variety of these supes but they mostly keep to themselves, rarely interacting with other species. There's always been a disdain amongst our kind. Some supernaturals are more powerful than others and stubbornness gets in the way.

This plan to unveil ourselves to the humans is truly a test. If we are unable to unite and get along—and I'm talking about more than one night—the humans won't accept us either.

We have to prepare for anything. It could be brilliant, or it could backfire on us. If we gain a human's trust, and reveal our life-changing secret, will they accept us or will they feel betrayed and hunt us down?

There could be war.

I have no doubt we'll find plenty of accepting humans. The ones who advocate for gender equality and don't condone genocide. Ones who have always believed but others saw them as crazy for doing so. Ones who read about fictional worlds involving the strange and unusual.

One problem we might run into are the people who've heard the urban legends that say supernatural beings are dangerous and evil. While we may have killed humans in the past, most of us did it to survive or in self-defense. It's not like that anymore. We are not a threat, aside from a few rogue supernatural beings who we make sure are caught and reprimanded immediately.

I take a place at the front and once the room is filled, a side door near the stage opens and Layla walks out, surrounded by her security team.

She's breathtaking in the violet puff sleeve dress with a sparkling full skirt. It complements her light brown skin, which fails to have that deathly vampire pallor to it. Her purple jeweled crown shines atop her curly mahogany hair.

I scan her body, despite most of her curves hidden by the fabric of the dress and imagine peeling it off so I can run my hands over her small breasts and rounded stomach, her thick thighs and meaty ass.

Layla's new gargoyle guard shifts on his feet behind her. His large hands are folded in front of his groin.

I take a moment to admire his beauty as well. He's taller than me, at least seven foot to my six foot three. He's massive. Thick arms that threaten to tear the short sleeves of his black tunic, tree trunk thighs stretching his pants and testing the seams. He has wings and a tail as I do but gargoyle tails can do marvelous things during sex.

An image flashes across my thoughts of the gargoyle fucking Layla while his tail fucks me, and *my* tail fills his asshole.

He shivers, as if I had broadcast that image to him, and runs a four-fingered, clawed hand over his scarred face. The urge to ask him how he got the mark surprises me into silence. It's not like me to care about another being's life story, but I want to know everything about this gargoyle. I still don't know his name, but I want to hear all about his adventures, his heartbreaks, what makes him happy.

Layla too.

Who are these magnificent creatures? Why are they affecting me so deeply?

I have an idea why I have this… extreme lust for the two, but I need to be certain.

An elder vampire named Cyrus, who is president of the council for the World Organization of Vampire Elites, enters from the same door Layla exited and walks onto the platform.

"Welcome, distinguished guests, to the first celebration hosted by Queen Layla Sophia Aldana," Cyrus says the moment he reaches the podium. He's nearly 900 years in age but appears no older than twenty-five. He has bleach blond hair, blue eyes, and a svelte build. "Tonight is more than just a party. Tonight is a chance at a new beginning for our world."

Raised voices fill the room, heads swiveling to neighbors for clarification of what the elder vampire could mean.

"For far too long, we've lacked unification amongst our kind. Let us change that. I encourage you all to mingle tonight, speak to a supe you would never naturally approach. We need to form allies, more cross-species support, especially as technology advances and it becomes harder and harder to conceal our identities."

I see a few supes nodding in agreement while others stare at the elder vamp with uncertain scowls.

I know exactly what Cyrus is doing. He's putting the idea inside their head that we need to work together for our future, for protection. Then once the committee is formed and the plan to reveal ourselves to humans is set, they'll break the news to the rest of the supernatural community.

It's brilliant, though secrets rarely survive in our community. There are too many creatures with advanced hearing listening.

Cyrus waits for the chatter in the room to subside before he continues.

"Tonight is the first step to a unified world. Now, if you'll please join me in welcoming Queen Aldana and gargoyle soldier, Thorne DuPont to the stage."

Thorne. Is he one of Xander's newer soldiers? There are many in his army, it's impossible to know all of them, but if this one is highly regarded enough to be selected to lead the new vampire queen's security team, I would have certainly met him by now.

Where have you been hiding?

Layla walks to the stage, Thorne following, but she stumbles going up the stairs. I have no doubt her vampire reflexes would have kicked in, but Thorne is just as fast and catches her. The moment his skin touches hers, a thrill of pleasure shoots through my middle and down to my cunt.

Oh.

Well.

That's interesting.

Chapter 4 - Layla

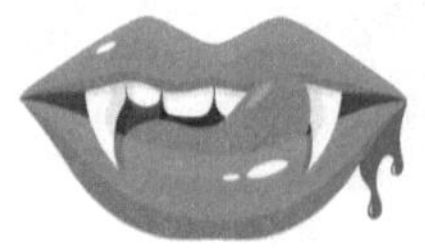

I t happened again.

Pleasure.

It rolls through me the moment Thorne grabs me by the waist with one arm to stop me from falling. His hand takes hold of my upper arm, and I swallow my moan. His smooth, velvety skin burns on mine. It's *intoxicating*.

The gargoyle's eyes widen. He feels it too.

My fangs unwillingly drop, and I quickly sheath them before anyone notices.

Once I'm upright, I smooth my dress to make sure I'm not flashing my tits and bits, and I can only hope my hair hasn't fallen out of place. I don't have a mirror to check it, and my phone is deep down in the pocket of this dress. It doesn't matter, though, because Thorne is already reaching out to push a curled strand off my cheek.

Heat simmers deep within my stomach, my nipples tightening at the affectionate move. I can only pray to whichever higher power is listening that the supernaturals in the room can't smell my needy pussy.

Of course, that's not the case based on the feverish look Vara is giving me from where she stands at the front—her fangs bared, pupils blown, breathing heavily.

I'm struggling to focus. I vaguely register Cyrus introducing Thorne as my new head of security, talking about our new partnership with the gargoyles and other supes who will be on my security team.

My mind races with filthy things I want to do to the sexy scarred gargoyle. But not just with him... with *Vara* too.

What the fuck?

It's clear the attraction I felt for Vara upon our first meeting a year ago hasn't waned.

I remember the moment we shook hands, my entire body lit up like a fucking Christmas tree. It was the first time I'd felt such *desire* for another soul since my short-lived love affair with Millie. I was left confused, also terrified, so I stayed away from the sphinx for the rest of the night... and for the past year. I know she felt something too because she's been begging Millie to bring me to one of her nightclubs. Or to take me out on a date. But she also respected my wishes and stayed away.

Now?

Thorne's touch is doing the exact same thing to my body: scorching my veins and awakening my sexual urges. How can someone I've only known for less than an hour cause such a reaction within me?

What if he's my mate?

I shake my head. In the nearly 700 years I've been undead; I've never heard of a vampire and a gargoyle being fated mates. Sure, vampires and gargoyles have hooked up—Millie and Locheran dated for a few months—but never have our souls been bound.

And then there's Vara...

Before my brain can even try to comprehend a second mate, Cyrus is done speaking, and I'm being whisked away into the crowd. I shake far too many hands—except for the fae, you never shake a fae's hand—and my face hurts from smiling at so many powerful supernaturals.

I've met them all many times before, including at my coronation. Even before I was crowned, they all knew me as Millie's royal advisor. Now it's different. Now I'm their equal.

Thorne hasn't left my side all night, but he's kept enough distance that we haven't touched again.

I desperately want him to touch me again.

My eyes also kept wandering over the crowd, searching for Vara. It's as if she sensed me seeking her out, locking eyes with me each time—the gold in them seemingly glowing.

The music changes to a slow song: *Wonderful Tonight* by Eric Clapton. The DJ has been playing a unique mix of music tonight, switching from songs of the 20th and 21st centuries to ones from hundreds of years ago. That's the thing about being immortal. We've experienced so much in our lifetime, from the changes in arts and culture to advancements in technology. We have to adapt so as not to out ourselves as supernaturals, even if that means learning lyrics to every Taylor Swift song but preferring to dance across a ballroom to Wolfgang Mozart's masterpieces.

With no one to dance with, I make my way off the dance floor—I still need to track down Xander to meet his new mate—but a clawed hand stops me.

Vara.

My breath hitches as her palm wraps around my forearm. It's warm and silken and my body threatens to melt beside her.

"Can I have this dance?"

I want to say no. I'm not much of a dancer. Well, no, that's a lie. I do well with choreographed dances or shaking

my ass in the middle of my living room to whatever pop-
ular song comes on the radio.

It's *slow* dancing that I'm not a fan of. Mostly because
of how intimate it is. How vulnerable I feel in another's
arms. Yet I'm eager to give Vara my hand.

She wraps her arm around me, tugging me against her
strong body. Because she's so tall, my eyes fall in line with
her plentiful breasts. Her hard nipples poke through the
silken fabric of her dress.

It's near intoxicating having her this close, her front
flush with mine and holding my hand as we sway to the
soothing notes of the song. I inhale deeply, Vara's cherry blossom scent entrancing me. My fangs drop and the
sphinx smirks, knowing exactly the effect she has on me.

Why did I run from her for so long?

I don't want to run anymore. Besides, why can't I have
a little fun? I'm the new vampire queen of New York City
after all. If I were a man, no one would bat an eye about
fucking around.

I place my palm on her back, just under where her wings
are attached, and spread out my fingers. The move causes
her tail to whip around behind her.

"Have I told you that you look magnificent tonight?"
Vara asks. My stomach tightens with desire at the sound
of her sultry voice.

"You haven't, but thank you."

"I take it you were told about my position?"

I wince, regretting how dismissive I was toward her when she crashed the meeting.

"Cyrus informed me shortly before going on stage." I sigh and swallow hard. "I'm sorry, Vara. I had no reason to be rude."

Vara's palm skates up and down my spine, and I shudder, stifling a whimper.

"One thing a queen should never be is sorry."

"Even queens make mistakes," I counter. "A good queen is one who can admit as such."

"Touché," she says, the word almost a purr. "I'm proud of you, though," she adds, and my praise kink stirs.

"For what?"

"For standing up to me. That rarely happens."

"It's the crown. It emboldens me." I shrug and avert my eyes.

Vara grips my chin and turns my head to look at her.

"It's not the crown, Layla. I crashed a meeting I wasn't invited to. I put my paws on you without your permission. I undermined your authority in front of others. I would have been disappointed had you *not* told me to fuck off. That crown is pretty, but it has no power. That's all you."

I giggle because she's right, but I won't tell her that. Can't let her already inflated ego grow.

We dance in silence, swaying in small circles. Vara's claws slowly scratch up and down my back, and each pass garners a shiver. My eyes find Thorne standing nearby watching us with heated attentiveness. His hands are covering his crotch.

Is he turned on too?

"You're trembling," Vara whispers.

I nod.

"Why?"

"I... I'm not sure."

"Are you shaking with need, Queen?"

My fangs cut into my bottom lip with how hard I'm struggling to hold back the moan that wants to pour from my lips. A drop of blood trickles onto my chin and Vara leans in to lap it up.

"Mmm. Delicious. Is your cunt as sweet as your blood?"

There's a low growl behind me, and I glance over my shoulder to see that Thorne has moved closer.

"The gargoyle is enjoying the show."

"He's my guard. Maybe he doesn't like how close you are to me."

A wicked smile spreads across Vara's face. She leans down and her lips graze against my ear, causing a shudder to roll through me.

"Or maybe the smell of your wet cunt is making him feral."

Thorne is up against my back now, trapping me between him and Vara.

What is happening?

His hands skim along my bare shoulders and arms. I lean into him, and he presses his hard cock into my back.

This is crazy.

Vara's claws dig into my hips, and she purrs, but it's not anything sweet like a house cat... it's full of possession and lust.

"Do you want him to fuck you?" Vara asks. She brushes her lips over mine, teasing me, torturing me.

I whimper. I didn't mean to, but yes... I do want Thorne to fuck me.

And I want Vara to join.

"Layla," Thorne nearly growls. His deep, rumbling voice only adds to the potent lust surging through my body. "We need to go. Now."

"What? Why?"

Panic nips at my nerves wondering if there's a threat that I missed while drooling over Vara and my new head of security.

"Because you're dripping." He's leaned over far enough to run his nose along my neck—quite the feat for him being so tall. His hands greedily paw at my breasts. Vara's hands smooth up and down my sides and if these two keep at it, I might just combust. "Every supernatural being in this room can smell that mouth-watering pussy. They won't stop staring. They're *hungry* for a taste, and I'm seconds away from ripping their eyes out for looking at what's ours."

Oh.

Fuck.

Why does that turn me on even more?

Wait.

"*Ours...*" I murmur. I want to argue that I belong to no one, especially controlling alpha men. Except, Thorne didn't say *mine*, he said *ours*.

"Ours," Vara confirms. "If you'll have us."

The song has long changed to a fast beat and while a few creatures dance around us, everyone else is watching the new vampire queen getting dry humped in the middle of the dance floor by a gargoyle and a sphinx.

"Now? Here?"

"Is that what you want?" Vara asks.

I'm not opposed to putting on a show and letting Vara and Thorne fuck me in front of a crowd.

"Greedy girl," Vara groans. "Isn't she being greedy, Thorne? Wanting the entire room to hear her moans, to see her come?"

Someone's tail wraps around my calf and tugs, spreading my legs apart. Then another tail slips in between. The moment the tip pushes my underwear aside and presses into my clit, I whimper.

Vara's large hand wraps around my throat. "Do you want us to claim you right now in front of everyone?"

The tail pressing into my clit starts vibrating, causing me to jolt.

It's Thorne's... because the tip of a gargoyle tail can do wonderful things like vibrate and expand... and self-lubricate.

"Y...y...yes." I can barely get the word out.

Vara smirks. "We'll give them one orgasm, then the rest are ours."

The tail that spread my legs is now nudging my entrance. I expect the tickling of her tuft, but instead, the tip of her tail has solidified.

No fucking way.

Vara swipes the teardrop tip through my wetness before she slides it inside me.

Thorne holds me in place, stopping me from falling to my knees. The pleasure from being fucked by a tail while another vibrates against my clit is intense and nothing like I've ever felt before.

"Such a good girl," Thorne growls against my ear.

I moan at the broody gargoyle's words. His lust seems to be bringing out his talkative side—filthy talk—and I can't get enough. He squeezes my breasts again before he slips one hand behind the top of my dress, pinching and pulling at one nipple. I lift my arm to clutch his neck.

Vara leans in, her hand still around my throat and her tail fucking me viciously and crashes her mouth over mine.

The kiss is soft, slow, *magnetic*.

She removes her hand only for it to be replaced by Thorne's. It's larger, stronger, and he squeezes hard enough to add mind-numbing pain to my pleasure. Vara's tongue continues to lash against mine and the moment the vibration of Thorne's tail intensifies, I explode with an orgasm.

The music playing does nothing to drown out my scream. I even hear other moans around the room, clearly reacting to the new vampire queen getting tail fucked in the middle of the dance floor.

Once my body stops shaking, Vara removes her tail and lifts the tip to Thorne's mouth.

He licks it clean.

Holy fuck.

"Come," Vara says, taking my hand and leading us off the dance floor. Thorne is behind me, holding my other hand.

Heads turn as we work our way through the crowd. Most of the beings here will party until the sun rises. There's no rule that says I must stay the entire night.

I spot Millie up against the wall, making out with Teddy. She comes up for air, eyes wide when we pass by, then she smirks and mouths, 'call me,' before wiggling her eyebrows.

I'm pretty sure she missed the show I just put on while taking part in her own public display of affection. Not that she would have disapproved. We've attended enough sex parties together in the seventies that a public fuck is nothing new or surprising for either of us.

Besides, just a few months ago, Millie let Teddy finger fuck her at The 27 Club before she claimed him with a bite.

But should I really be doing this? Thorne is my new head of security. He's supposed to protect me, not fuck me. Will I need to fire him after tonight? Not to mention that I don't know a thing about him. We literally just met. How old is he? What's his favorite color? Favorite food?

Same with Vara. Though I know more about her since she's a prominent supe, owning most of the supernatural nightclubs in New York City. Her last name is Gamal. She's old too, at least 2,000, but she's still a stranger.

I mean, I've had plenty of threesomes with strangers before. Orgies too. But tonight feels different. I'm eager and on edge.

You know what?

Fuck it.

I've already had Vara's tail inside me and Thorne's hands on my breasts.

I want more.

As we leave the room, no one stares back with judgment. If anything, they appear envious or impressed. They don't care that the new queen will bed two lovers tonight.

Then why should I care?

I deserve this.

Vara leads us down the hallway, exiting the building to a waiting limo. I didn't request the extravagant ride but it's what they gave me tonight. Three vampires follow us outside—since I'm vampire queen and can't go anywhere without a protection detail.

Thorne instructs them to follow us in the SUV parked behind the limo before reaching out his hand to help me inside.

"Tell us what you need, Layla," Vara mewls, shutting the door behind her.

The moment the driver takes off towards my penthouse, Thorne grabs me and moves me around like I'm a doll and not a 200 pound woman. He lays me down on the seat that runs the length of the limo and takes his place at my head while Vara slides between my legs.

She bunches up the fabric of my dress, piling it in my middle.

"You've soaked these panties, my darling," she groans and peels them off.

Balling them up in her hands, she lifts them to her nose and inhales with her entire body. Once she's done, she hands them to Thorne and he does the same thing, responding with a growl.

That's sexy as hell.

Is this happening? Am I really about to be fucked by these two gorgeous monsters?

Vara's fur-covered hand smooths up my inner thigh until her fingertips tease my slick opening. I've noticed she's retracted her claws so as not to injure me.

Not that it matters, I'd heal immediately. Maybe I'll tell her to keep the claws out next time.

Next time?

This time has barely begun, yet I already want it to happen again.

"Tell us what you want us to do to you," Vara repeats.

"I want you both to touch me."

Vara smirks and nods to Thorne. "Play with those glorious tits."

Thorne complies. His four-fingered hands push away the top of the dress, exposing my breasts. When Vara slides a finger inside me, Thorne pinches both of my nipples. My back arches off the seat and I moan, loud enough that any supernatural within a mile of us likely heard.

"Our needy queen is so vocal, isn't she, Thorne?"

He doesn't respond, instead, he replaces his fingers with his mouth, taking an aching nipple between his teeth and lapping his tongue over the tip.

"Fuck," I groan.

"Already so close, aren't you, Layla-bug? This tight little cunt is choking my finger so good right now," Vara says, then adds a second finger.

A *thick* finger because her hands are like a lion's paw.

"Take Thorne's cock out of his pants like a good girl and let him fuck your mouth."

Vara's demands combined with her praise nearly have me coming right then, but I do as I'm told and reach above my head. Thorne guides my hands until my fingertips graze the stretchy band of his pants.

I pull down and his bulbous cock springs free.

No wonder he kept covering his groin all night. He had no resistance to keep his lust intact.

"No underwear? Aren't you a naughty gargoyle?" Vara croons, voicing my thoughts.

Her mouth descends on my clit, and I buck and scream when she sucks on it like a *lollipop*.

I'm bursting with desire as my small, trembling hands wrap around Thorne's length. I fist him, pumping up and down, squeezing just enough to garner a whimper from him.

Fuck. I love when men are vocal during sex.

He shudders and moans when I wrap my lips around his tip, and his pleasure rolls through me. Vara also groans while eating me out.

I'm not going to last long.

A light buzzing noise fills the limo, and I glance down my body to find Thorne's tail has slipped underneath Vara's dress.

"I want to see," I say.

Vara doesn't need me to explain. She lifts her dress enough to show the end of Thorne's tail pressed up against her clit.

"Let Thorne fuck your mouth, Layla-cakes," Vara says, her voice strained with pleasure.

I part my lips enough for Thorne to gently slide in, all the way to the back of my throat.

Thank goodness for no gag reflex.

Closing my mouth around Thorne, he starts pumping in and out of me, cautiously.

"She won't break, Thorne baby. Let her have it."

And that he does. He pulls out, then thrusts back in roughly with a grunt. His eyes fall to mine, and I give him a small nod to urge him to keep going.

Vara's mouth returns to my clit, and she resumes fucking me with two of her girthy fingers. She's moaning from her own stimulation, which causes *me* to moan around Thorne's cock.

The pleasure is overwhelming, and I'm the first to erupt with an orgasm. Vara follows a few minutes later and once she removes her fingers from my pussy, Thorne picks up his speed.

Vara crawls to him and shoves her fingers, coated with my pleasure, into Thorne's mouth. He sucks them eagerly—as if he hadn't just tasted me on the dance floor—and I moan at the sight.

After a few more rough pumps, the gargoyle comes, emptying himself down my throat.

And fuck, it's a lot of cum.

Thorne removes his heavy cock from my mouth once he's done and collapses onto the seat, breathing heavily. My head falls to his lap, and he combs his fingers through my hair. Vara sits on the limo's floor, her head resting on my stomach.

"That was beautiful," she says.

I hum with no words to describe what we just did.

"Fucking fantastic," Thorne says and for some reason, hearing a curse from the broody gargoyle who doesn't speak a lot makes me laugh.

My giggles cause Vara to join in and even Thorne chuckles.

After nearly a minute of losing our minds to post-sex bliss, the driver uses the intercom to announce our arrival to my penthouse.

"Now," Vara begins, adjusting her dress and fixing mine so we're both fully covered. "You've got a busy day tomorrow. A busy week, to be honest."

"You're leaving?" I didn't mean to sound so needy.

Vara smiles and palms my cheek.

"Don't worry, we *will* be doing this again, but you need your rest."

She glances up at Thorne.

"You'll stay with her?"

He nods and Vara pats his cheek too.

"Good boy."

With that, she slips out of the limo and flies away.

Chapter 5 - Thorne

In the 712 years I've been alive, I've never had sex like that.

Encompassing. *Intense.*

The amount of cum I shot down Layla's throat would have drowned her if she were mortal. It's not like I was backed up. I still take my cock by hand when bored or stressed or just needing release. But seeing her find pleasure in my pleasure, watching as Vara made Layla moan with just her fingers and tongue, acted as a catalyst and my body exploded with an orgasm.

My cock is already getting hard again reliving the moment.

Fuck, this is a bad idea. I shouldn't be fucking the new vampire queen.

"You really are the definition of broody, huh?" Layla says as we enter her building.

"I'm afraid I let my thoughts win far too often."

She frowns but doesn't question what I mean.

Before the ball, Layla gave me a packet with information on the security at her building. The high-rise has been overhauled with new protocols, including the most up-to-date technologies. I also notice plenty of security guards as we pass. Most of them are supernatural beings masked from the human world.

The two middle-aged humans manning the lobby desk glance up when we walk by, their eyes widening at the team of large men surrounding Layla. No, that's not why they appear so shocked. They've likely seen her walk in with her bodyguards plenty of other times before. It's me. I'm in my human form, but I resemble a seven-foot-tall muscular man who looks as if he could break a neck with a pinky finger.

My pinky finger isn't like a human's. It's thick and clawed and strong.

I bet Layla's pinky finger is adorable. When we get to the well of elevators and wait for one to open, I take her hand and lift it to inspect the tiny thing. Sure enough, her pinky is dainty as fuck.

"What are you doing, Thorne?" Layla asks. A smile lights up her face, and my heart does a little dance at the fact that she finds me amusing, which never happens.

I'm not a funny guy.

"Your hand. It's cute."

An elevator in the middle dings and we all pile in. I extract my access card to the penthouse and tap it to the reader. After pressing the penthouse button, the elevator rises.

Layla puffs out a laugh. "My hand is... cute?"

"Yes. Look." I grab her hand and place it against my palm. "See how tiny and adorable it is compared to mine?"

She tilts her head, examining the size difference. She bites her lip, and the scent of her arousal hits my nose.

Is she thinking about what my large hands and thick fingers could do to her?

Wait... if I can smell her sweet sex, then so can these vampire guards. I growl, and they seem to understand the threat and back away as far as they can.

"So protective," Layla whispers, followed by a giggle.

"It *is* what I was chosen to do."

The elevator dings again, announcing our arrival at the penthouse. I instruct the three vampires to enter first and conduct a quick sweep of the place. While Layla and I wait, I admire the small foyer to her home. The cream marble floors are streaked with gold throughout. Along the wall to the right is a wooden table with a statue of a naked woman on top. A Renaissance painting of an orgy hangs on the wall above it.

This sexual little vamp... I think about Vara's words.

We'll do this again.

I can't wait to be inside her again. It may not happen right away, especially with all the meetings and appearances Layla is scheduled to attend. But I'm eager. Will she let me fuck her while my tail takes her up her ass? Will Vara order us around again? I can be dominant, but I *love* submitting to a powerful woman.

"Thorne," Layla whispers, her fangs drop, and her eyes turn black. Something I notice happens when she's turned on. "You growled again."

I wince. I'm not a growler. Even when I'm angry and want to appear threatening, I stay silent and intimidating. It works for me.

It's Layla... Vara too. Just the thought of us all together again makes me feral.

The vampire guards return, giving us the all clear. I snap out of it when Layla grabs my hand and pulls me through a set of heavy oak doors into her apartment.

She's... she's holding my hand. Why is my head swimming and my heart thrashing inside my chest over this simple act of affection?

Layla doesn't appear to be affected by holding my hand as she gives me a tour. Her penthouse is cozy yet modern with sleek furniture and décor, mixed with items that would now be considered antiques.

A beautiful console table with intricate golden designs along the legs and topped with a white and gray marble lines a hallway wall. Beside it is a Windsor Cherry grandfather clock with an arm ticking back and forth. Next to the clock, hanging on the wall, is an ornate gold framed mirror that looks slightly haunted.

Ghosts are real but they don't like to haunt supernaturals. We don't fall for their bullshit pranks—a book levitating off a table? Lights flickering? Changing the room's temperature? Witches can do all of that with their magic. Humans are far more gullible, which is why ghosts find them more entertaining.

Layla's living room is encased by windows overlooking the Empire State Building—which is lit up in purple and gold tonight. A white sectional couch sits in front of a long electric fireplace in the wall with a flat-screen TV mounted above. On the opposite side of the room is quite the collection of books and trinkets spanning centuries.

They sit on shelves of bookcases that look like they came from that one store with the really good meatballs.

The hallway leading to the bedrooms is simple with only a few paintings hung throughout. It's also narrower than the hallway just inside the entrance, so no tables line these walls. We pass by a few doors that I assume are guest rooms, until arriving at the main bedroom. It's decorated with dark purple painted walls and gold accents throughout.

Certainly, it's a coincidence that the purple matches my skin, and the gold resembles Vara's wings and fur?

The bedding on her king-sized bed is white and there are too many pillows for me to count. She has a white, antique vanity along one wall next to a matching antique dresser. A purple chaise lounge sits in a corner with a small table in front of it. Stacks of romance books are on top.

I want to flip through the pages and read what brings her joy, but she's already leading me back out into the hallway.

When we reach the kitchen, she releases my hand. I already miss her cold touch.

"Would you like something to drink? I don't have much since I rarely entertain anymore." Layla opens the fridge and peers in. "Let's see... there's wine and water. I might have a bottle of whiskey or vodka somewhere."

I've never been a heavy drinker, and I wouldn't want anything that could impair me while I'm working.

Though it would take quite a lot of booze to make gargoyles even slightly tipsy. The buzz doesn't last long either. Drinking water will take the fun away pretty quickly. I believe it's because we're meant to protect and doing so impaired is not feasible, so our bodies work overtime to sober us up as fast as possible.

"Just water please."

She nods and spins around, using her vampire speed to fill a glass with ice and water from the spout on the fancy fridge. It's one that has an electronic display on the door. Her entire kitchen is fancy: several feet of marble countertops and spacious white cabinets, a stove with six burners on top, a wine fridge, a double sink with an expandable faucet.

I sit on a stool at the massive island, which could easily fit eight, maybe ten, people around it.

"Why don't you entertain anymore?"

She hands me the water and wiggles her nose, once again reminding me of an adorable bunny.

"It's been a while since I've found anyone worth entertaining. Millie and I used to go out all the time, but it started to feel too repetitive. We'd go to a club, dance and get drunk off boozed blood, we'd find someone to fuck, then do it all over the next week."

"You and Millie were an item, right?"

It's what I've heard some of my fellow gargoyle soldiers gossiping about.

She snorts. "First of all, no one describes romantic relationships as 'an item' anymore."

I shrug, accepting I will always be a socially awkward gargoyle who says all the wrong things.

"But, yes, Millie and I were together. We met in New Orleans in 1921. She was the closest I ever felt to being in love."

"Not even when you were human?"

Layla frowns, likely at whatever memory I just triggered.

"When I was human, I was married, but I never loved my husband. How could I when it was an arranged marriage: my life in exchange for more land, a higher status in society. It's just how things worked back then. I was only fourteen, for fuck's sake, ten years younger than my husband. He abused me from day one, physically and mentally, any chance he got. He only saw me as a breeding mule, but there was something wrong with my body. I wasn't able to get pregnant, which pissed him off even more."

The anger that rolls through my body is palpable. Layla senses it and reaches out to take my hand. I should be the one consoling her! I attempt to reel in my fury hearing about her abusive husband, despite it happening centuries ago and there's nothing I can do about it now.

Except be here for her.

She gently squeezes my hand and continues.

"I was thirty-two when I became a vampire. It was 1348, and I lived in a small town in The Crown of Castile or what is now modern-day Spain. I'd fallen sick with the bubonic plague, though we had called it The Black Death because the disease wiped out entire towns. I was ready to face my end. To end my suffering at my husband's hands. It's something I never told Millie. She believes I was thankful to be turned. At the time, I wasn't. I wanted to be at peace. Now that I'm immortal, I'm making the best of this long life."

"I think we all are, honestly," I offer.

She smiles. "Yes, well, it was still a life forced on me by a possessive man who didn't want to lose me. Rumors of immortal creatures swirled for years, and the moment I became sick, my husband sought one to save me. It didn't take long. A vampire named Diago had been watching me for weeks after spotting me one night walking home from the market. He'd become quite obsessed with me, so when my husband begged Diago to turn me, basically selling my soul to this supernatural being, he gladly agreed."

"What happened to your husband?" I ask.

A wicked smile spreads across her face and my cock jumps. She transformed from bunny to beast within seconds. Vampires have a history of being dangerous... ruth-less. I never saw that with Layla until now.

"When I turned, I needed human blood to complete the process. So, I drained my husband—not a drop left. Feeling his life fade, his heartbeat slowing, was invigorating. I knew at that moment I was a monster. Instead of being upset or angry about being turned, I quickly saw it as an opportunity to take control. A second chance."

Her words cut off and the vindictive smile fades. I sense there's more to her story, but the way she shuts down as if flipping a switch tells me story time is over.

I go to take a drink of my water and find the glass empty. Damn, I was parched. I stand to get more, but the next thing I know, the glass is out of my hand and Layla is refilling it.

"I guess pouring all that cum down my throat can make you dehydrated," she says with a laugh.

My cheeks heat, my heart flutters, and my cock jerks.

"Oh," Layla chirps, covering her mouth. Fucking supernatural hearing busting me and my lust. "I didn't mean to... um... rile you up."

I take another drink of water to stop myself from saying something embarrassing.

"I like hearing your heart react to me," she says.

I stare at the glass of water, twisting it around on the countertop. "Do you not fuck humans? Or supes who have heartbeats?"

I cringe the moment I ask the questions.

"Sorry, that's none of my business."

"It's fine." Layla smiles, relaxing her tense shoulders. "I do fuck beings with heartbeats, but it's been a while. I just forgot how fascinating and sensitive the little organs are. Yours is very... active."

She giggles, probably remembering how chaotic my heartbeat was when we first met.

It's chaotic right now.

I should change the subject.

"So, um, I have some things I'd like to discuss," I say, standing to extract my phone so I can take notes.

Layla's face transforms to delight.

I tilt my head.

She covers her mouth again. Why does she keep hiding her joy?

"Sorry. I got excited."

"About me wanting to discuss things with you?"

"Yeah. I like hearing you talk. Your voice is so deep and sexy. Xander said you're a gargoyle of few words, but I think you're warming up to me. I need more."

Fuck I'm blushing again.

She waves her hand, shaking her head. "Sorry, please go on."

"Um, right, so your security detail... I'd like to double your guards. That way, you can have two always stationed outside your penthouse doors. I counted three manning the lobby, which is good, but I'd like four additional guards patrolling the perimeter of your building at all times. When you're on the move, out in public, there will always be two to four guards by your side. I'll rotate them out every day so we don't fall into a routine."

"Change them out?" Her eyes widen, panic filling them. "Does that mean you won't be with me?"

She's moved to sit on a stool next to where I stand and reaches out to place her hand on my forearm. I shudder at her touch and cover her knuckles with my palm.

"I will be there whenever you need me."

She relaxes immediately. Ok... so maybe she is as affected by me as I am by her.

This isn't a good idea.

What was I thinking fooling around with the woman I'm supposed to be protecting? This desire that's consuming my thoughts and body has already been distracting. I can't have distractions when my job is to keep the new vampire queen alive.

I dip my head to hide my concern.

"A few of your guards will share units in the building, that way they're close and ready if a threat presents itself. We should also get a witch in here to ward the place. And I'd like someone to stay here inside the penthouse with you, especially now that you'll be heading this committee for the unveiling plan. If word gets out before you're ready for the supe community to know, I worry you'll get unwanted attention or even threats."

She opens her mouth, but I raise my hand.

"I don't think it should be me." She frowns, questions on the tip of her tongue. "I will stay here tonight, as I promised Vara, but after that, I'll reside in another apartment in the building. What we did on the dance floor... and in the limo... I can't let that distract me from protecting you. I already like you way too much—"

"You like me?" Layla asks, a smile spreading across her beautiful face.

"Yes, and I worry that if I stay here, we'll never leave your bedroom."

"That's okay—"

"It's not okay. In fact, it's a bad idea."

"Rude," Layla grumbles with a pout, crossing her arms.

"You know what I mean. You can't have distractions either. You're not only the new vampire queen, but now you have this committee to lead. It's a lot of responsibility."

That adorable bunny nose scrunches as my words sink in. She knows I'm right.

"Fine. I guess I see your point," she says and sighs.

Layla grabs her phone to look at the time.

"We still have a few hours before sunrise. Do you want to watch a movie?"

I pause before answering because I literally just had this thought—how all I want to do is cuddle on a couch with someone and watch a movie. I try to remember the last time I let myself enjoy the company of another being.

It's been too long.

Even on my nights off, I'm typically out walking the city, sitting in the park reading a book, or going to a nightclub that Locheran drags me to. I'll watch documentaries by myself, but sitting on a couch, curled up with another being, while some cheesy rom-com plays is not something I've done before.

Layla's smile falters at my hesitation. "Right. Bad idea."

"It *is* a bad idea."

"And it's not part of your job description..." She bites her lip, her thoughts clearly turning mischievous. "But neither is having your cock in my mouth so..."

I narrow my eyes at her, and she holds up her hands in innocence.

"Fine," I relent. "One movie."

She claps and turns to her cabinets. Her excitement for such a mundane activity makes me wonder just *how* long it's been since she's entertained. Does Millie no longer come over for a girls' night? A movie night? Just to hang out? I suppose the former vampire queen has been preoccupied the past couple of months with her new fated mate.

Layla excuses herself and disappears out of the kitchen at vampire speed and is gone for less than a minute before she returns, now dressed in an over-sized t-shirt and baggy pants. She pours herself a glass of wine, and I refill my water then join her in the living room where she scrolls through movie and TV titles on a streaming app.

"Oooh," she says, finding something that piques her interest. "*Is It Cake?*! Have you ever watched this?"

She turns her head, biting her lip, anticipating my answer.

"No."

That was the right thing to say because she nearly jumps with joy.

"It's so good. These bakers make cakes, but the cakes resemble different objects, like a suitcase or a shoe or a stuffed animal, and they have to trick the judges into thinking it's real!"

Her words are fast in her excitement, and I'm not sure I understand the gist of the show, but she presses play and sits in the middle of her white sectional couch. She pats the cushion next to hers.

When I hesitate, she pouts. "I'll be good, I promise."

Fuck, I'm in trouble.

I'm struggling to resist this woman.

When I sit, she leans into me, and I instinctively wrap my arm around her shoulders.

You know what? Fuck bad ideas.

I need this.

I can worry about my rules tomorrow.

The cake show is better than I expected and most of the time, I couldn't tell what was real and what was cake. When the second episode starts playing, Layla's eyes begin to droop. I unfurl my wings and wrap them around her. She burrows deeper into my side and within minutes, she's asleep.

I carefully lift her off the couch and carry her to the main bedroom at the back. The sun is rising, and her UV protection shades lower. I tuck her in and when I walk away, she says my name.

"Thank you for staying."

She falls back asleep and despite how badly I want to crawl into bed with her, I force myself to walk down the hallway to a guest bedroom.

I dream about Layla.

And Vara.

Chapter 6 - Layla

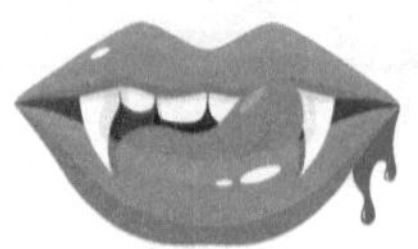

I wake up a few minutes after sunset to a note from Thorne letting me know he had to grab some things from his place. He'd told me there were three available units in my building, and he'll be moving into one of them so he can stay close to me.

But not too close.

Whatever.

I understand. He has a job. No distractions. No bad ideas.

It's not like I need a guard staying in my penthouse with me anyway. Millie never had that when she was queen. Thorne said it's a precaution because of the unification plan.

I think he's being overprotective.

But I kinda like it.

When he returns, I've already fed on a donor and dressed for the night.

"Ready to go?" I ask when I walk out of my bedroom and into the living area where Thorne is standing, looking out the window while talking on his phone.

He turns at my voice and stumbles over his words. I'm not even paying attention to what he's saying, because all I care about is how his eyes rake over my body. How his tail whips back and forth behind him, his wings fluttering from their position against his back.

It's amazing how gargoyle wings work. They're known to have a ten-foot spread. Yet when Thorne's are flush against his back, they seem so small, likely to stay out of the way when not in use.

"I'll talk to you later," Thorne says, ending his call. He stuffs the phone in his pants pocket.

"Ready to go?" I repeat, only this time the words come out breathy... a whisper.

Thorne stalks toward me, stopping just a foot away. I fight the urge to reach out for him.

"You look beautiful," he says, checking me out again.

I'm wearing a black sleeveless blouse that has a dipped neckline, tucked into my white high waist trousers.

He lifts his hand, then stops after realizing what he's doing.

"Don't stop," I beg.

He lifts it again to palm my cheek. I close my eyes and lean into his touch. It's so warm. Burning, almost. I don't think that has anything to do with me being undead with cold skin. Gargoyles must run hotter. Thorne is like a furnace and all I want to do is hold him, cuddle with him. He reminds me of when I was human, and I'd sit in front of the fireplace on a snowy night while reading a beautiful love story.

But before I can enjoy this moment, Thorne drops his hand and curses, turning away from me.

"I can't. I want to, Gods do I want to, but I can't. We can't."

He stands there, breathing roughly, trying to compose himself. After a few moments of silence, I say, "I know. I'm sorry."

"Don't be sorry. Please." He pivots enough to see me. "I'm the one who's not strong enough. If I start, I won't be able to stop."

I'm not opposed to that. I don't say the words out loud, though, because Thorne is doing everything he can to resist this pull between us.

He's being good. He's just trying to do his job.

I'm the one being naughty.

We leave the penthouse and head down to WOVE headquarters in Lower Manhattan to go over additional candidates to join my security team. Thorne sits in the front seat of the SUV, leaving two vampire guards in the back with me.

I sulk about it the entire drive.

When we get to the conference room, Thorne sits on the other side of the table, again distancing himself from me.

Oh, okay. He's *serious*.

After an hour of going over portfolios, we chose our first round of candidates and called them all for interviews. Luckily, most of them were able to meet today, likely expecting our calls since the vampire elders and other supes have been planning this collaboration for months.

The first interview is with a young shifter named Daniel. He's around fifty immortal years, but he appears no older than someone in their mid-twenties. He's muscular throughout, but not nearly as beefy as Thorne.

I don't think many supes could match Thorne's physique.

Daniel is extremely flirty as we ask him questions. Well, Thorne is asking the questions, but Daniel looks at me when answering. He even gives me a few smile-filled winks, his blue eyes twinkling with mischief. His blond hair falls in shaggy waves around his head.

He's handsome, but I'm not attracted to him.

"Thank you for your interest," Thorne says suddenly. "We'll call if you're selected."

Daniel looks at me as if I'll go against Thorne's words. I shrug and wave to dismiss him.

"Thorne, he sounded great," I say the moment the shifter is out the door.

"I didn't like the way he looked at you."

"And how did he look at me?"

"Like he wanted to fuck you."

I roll my eyes. "He did not. He was a sweet guy. It was an innocent flirt."

"Nothing is innocent when it comes to men," he says, standing to toss Daniel's file in the trash can sitting in the corner of the room.

I scoff and stand too. "You're a man."

"I'm a gargoyle."

"And gargoyles don't do bad things?"

"We do."

I pinch the bridge of my nose. "Okay, but if you say no to potential guards just because they smile or flirt with me, then we'll have no one to hire."

He ignores my concern and cracks the door open to call for the next candidate.

A griffin named Erebos walks in on all fours, his tail whipping back and forth. Thorne moves the chairs out of the way for him to sit, perched at the table like a lion gazing out over his pride.

His eagle head rotates nearly 360 degrees as he scans the room. His talons tap on the linoleum floor and his beak snaps open and shut. All actions of a guard surveying his surroundings and assessing those in his presence.

Thorne sits taller, his face filled with pride. I can tell he already likes this one, but I tune out the interview because Erebos is rather boring, nearly as serious and broody as Thorne. He doesn't flirt with me, in fact, he doesn't even address me other than the original greeting. He's far more interested in engaging Thorne with warrior speak. At least, that's what I called it because after answering questions pertaining to the security role, Thorne and Erebos compared war stories for at least ten minutes.

We made it through two more candidates with no flirty issues when a werewolf walks in. The man, whose name is Carigan, is about 200 years in age, but appears no older than forty. He has short black hair and brown eyes and medium brown skin. He's tall, about six three, if I were to guess, and massive. Not muscular like Thorne. The were is wide and soft, reminding me of a wrestler.

He's intimidating but sweet and smiles nonstop. It's infectious, and I find myself smiling back.

Which only pisses Thorne off, garnering a growl.

Fuck, I love when Thorne growls. It's so animalistic and possessive. My nipples are already hardening, thinking about all the other wonderful sounds he makes, especially the ones when I had his cock in my mouth.

Thorne stills, Carigan's nostrils flair, and I swear I hear a muffled howl.

Werewolves can't change at will like shifters, but their inner monster is still sentient between full moons. It still *craves*.

Thorne has Carigan by the throat and against the wall within seconds. He bares his fangs, his claws digging into the were's skin.

"Thorne, release him immediately," I command, my own fangs out.

"I'm sorry, man," Carigan wheezes, Thorne's grip on his neck nearly crushing his vocal box. "I didn't mean to... um... to smell her."

"Let him go, Thorne. That's an order!"

Thorne hesitates, only for a second, before he releases the poor supe.

"I apologize, Carigan. We'll... call you."

If he'll even want to be part of the team after Thorne tried to kill him, which I have no doubt would have happened if I hadn't stopped him.

When Carigan leaves, I walk to where Thorne stands. Anger radiates from his body, his clawed hand opening and closing into fists.

"You can't do that, Thorne!" I say, shoving at his chest. He stumbles back at the force. "You could have killed him and—"

Thorne cuts off my words by grabbing my hips and lifting me onto the conference room table. He clutches my head in his hands and descends on me with a rough but passionate kiss. His plump lips work my mouth eagerly until it opens, allowing his tongue to slip through.

I whimper as Thorne grinds his bulge into my cloth-covered pussy. I bury my hands into his hair, which he has up in a knot at the top of his head. I tug at the strands, and he growls against my lips.

"Please," I moan as he moves his lips to my chin and down my neck.

He lays me back on the table to continue moving his greedy mouth down my chest and stomach. I part my legs, ready for him to tear these pants off my body. To bury his head in my sex. To taste me and fuck me with his tongue.

But a knock at the door snaps Thorne out of this shot of lust.

"Fuck," he groans against my fupa.

I'm about to tell him to ignore whoever is outside the door but the knob turns, and we scramble to right ourselves before it opens fully.

The next candidate—who definitely notices our disheveled appearances and our swollen lips—walks in.

"Is this a perk of the job?" the fae warrior smirks.

"Absolutely fucking not," Thorne says with a huff before marching out of the room.

I smile at the woman with pale skin, silver eyes, and stark white hair. She's wearing a black tank top and faux leather pants—clothes that barely contain her short yet muscular body.

"He'll be back. He just needs a moment."

"I'm sure he does."

Chapter 7 - Layla

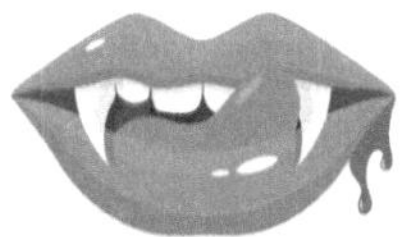

It's been a week since the party and possibly the best sex of my life. Vara hasn't been around, and Thorne has barely spoken to me, let alone touched me, since the day he lost control while interviewing candidates for my security team.

When he returned to the room, he brought in two other guards. Assurances so we wouldn't be alone together.

The next day—with the same two guards babysitting us—we went over all the candidates we interviewed and liked and made our final choices. My team will have fifty guards total, thirty who will be on duty at night and the rest will keep watch during the day, rotating shifts to allow each guard to have at least two days off.

Most of my team consists of vampires with griffins, shifters, werewolves—including Carigan, who surprisingly accepted the job when Thorne offered it to him—and a handful of witches mixed in. Thorne also hired Isa, the fae warrior, which I found interesting that a fae even wanted the job since they're selfish creatures.

A vampire guard was assigned to stay in one of my guest rooms. The young vamp takes his job seriously and barely talks to me, which is fine because I've been in a bad mood.

I'm cranky because I'm frustrated and horny as fuck and it feels as if I'm going to suddenly combust if I don't get some relief. Even my trusty vibes haven't been able to help.

The only thing that's kept my mind off... *them,* is the fact that I've been busy with meetings and appearances.

The day after selecting my security team, I met with supernatural leaders from across all species to discuss who will be representing them on the committee for the Supernatural Unveiling Plan. Supes who can't emerge at night, or are bound to their environments for whatever reason, were included via video conference.

Another day, I spent handing out sentences to vampires for violating our laws. Most were minor infractions, but a handful were major, like breaking our compulsion rules:

No compelling for sexual pleasure.

No compelling a human to commit a crime.

No repeat compelling as it could cause brain damage.

Another day, I met with concerned vampires about various things like the lack of blood donors—there are only hundreds compared to the thousands of vampires in New York City. I'm hoping that number will go up with humans volunteering after learning about our existence.

Last night, I had a networking event with human politicians: A fundraiser for a children's charity that I donated a million dollars to—some of my money, most from WOVE. The moment Thorne spotted me in my red strapless dress, he marched out of my penthouse and Erebos arrived to let me know he'd be escorting me.

Thorne set a boundary between us, but I could see how desperately he wanted to break his rules. It's why he limited how often he'd escort me to meetings or wait outside of the room, away from me, while another guard stood inside in his place.

It's as if the more he held out, the more frustrated and agitated he became.

Now it's Friday, and tonight is the first meeting for SUC—I chuckle at the irony of the acronym for Supernatural Unveiling Committee being SUC since vampires literally suck blood from necks.

I slip on a pair of high-waisted black trousers and a purple short-sleeve blouse. My loose curls have been tamed in a ponytail with a few ringlets framing my face. I add a gold necklace with a simple purple diamond and matching gold hoop earrings to complete my look before turning and leaving my bedroom.

I nearly stop in my tracks when I spot Thorne in my living room, sitting on my couch with one leg propped on his knee reading the romance book I'd left on the coffee table last night.

Oh, God... which part is he at? Some of my romance books are absolutely vile. I fucking love them though.

He closes the book—one of my mafia romances—and sets it down on the table. Thorne reading is sexy as fuck, but Thorne potentially reading about a knife play scene between rivals has my fangs wanting to drop.

I manage to control my lust and head to the kitchen. Thorne stands and follows, hands tucked in the pockets of his black cargo pants. I scan his body, trying not to drool over the way his muscles stretch the black short-sleeved tunic he's wearing.

His long black hair falls around his face and over his broad chest.

Goddamn he's sexy.

He smiles, flashing me his fangs. His wings are tucked to his back as usual, but they flutter as he checks me out. His tail also reacts, whipping back and forth behind him.

"You look beautiful. Powerful."

I dip my head and smile, but Thorne reaches out, clutching my chin and lifting it back up. I ignore the way my body lights up when his skin touches mine.

"Why do you always do that?"

"Do what?"

"Hide your joy."

My brows pinch, not understanding.

"When you laugh, you cover your mouth. When you smile, you look away or look down at your feet."

Oh. I didn't realize...

"Please don't hide your smile. It's like a bright light in a room blanketed in darkness," Thorne says, his voice soft and quiet. "And your laughter..."

His words trail off, his eyes widening. He drops his hand, as if realizing he was about to cross that boundary line again.

"What is it?"

He shakes his head.

I'm about to demand he tell me about my laughter because how do you just say something like that but refuse to finish your sentence?! The broody mother fucker. When I open my mouth to yell at him, a guard interrupts to let us know the driver is here. Thorne is already on the move, opening the penthouse door for me.

The town car is silent as we head to WOVE headquarters. Thorne stares out the window while *I* stare at him.

He sighs and turns his head to me.

"Yes, my queen?"

I hadn't expected him to address me so formally, and I scrunch my nose, which makes him grin.

Getting a grin from Thorne is like striking gold!

"So, are you done avoiding me?"

"I wasn't—"

"You absolutely were, like the fucking plague. No, I lived through the plague. Even the rats got more attention than me."

He scrubs his hands over his face. "I'm sorry, Layla. I needed some distance. I've been struggling to control my urges around you."

"Have they been controlled then?"

"No, and I'm pretty sure staying away from you made it worse."

I let his words sink in, only the sounds of the city outside filling the quiet interior of the SUV. There's really only one explanation as to why we're both having these intense reactions to one another. Why we're both in physical pain when apart. But I'm struggling to believe that the three of us are mates.

"Well, I'm glad you're back," I finally say to Thorne.

I'm also relieved. My chest has been tight for the past week. Just having Thorne here now, sitting next to me in this SUV, feels as if whatever weight that was crushing my chest has been lifted.

Well, not entirely. There's still a pressure there. As if my undead heart is attempting to come to life, digging into my sternum and trying to escape.

No doubt for my missing piece.

Trying to find Vara.

"Tell me about my laughter," I demand, needing to change the subject.

"What?"

"You said my smile could light up a room blanketed in darkness and my laughter..."

I wave my hand around as if that would help him spit it out.

"I have no idea what you're talking about," he says, still giving me that heart-stopping grin—good thing I'm already dead.

"You're not going to gaslight me, buddy. Tell me or I'll... I'll..."

"You'll what, Layla?"

He raises a brow, challenging me.

I wish I still had my knife to stab him. When I was Millie's advisor, I'd keep it holstered to my hip. It's infused

with a witch's spell that can incapacitate most supernatural beings. Sadly, it's frowned upon for a queen to carry
weapons.

"Fine. I have nothing to threaten you with, but I *need* to
know, Thorne. Pleeeaaassse."

I know I'm being childish, I even pout and give him
puppy dog eyes, but I can't help it. The gargoyle is *killing*
me!

He narrows his eyes but relents.

"Your laughter is cute. Contagious."

"No!"

I punch him in the shoulder; he even pretends it hurts.
He tilts his head and smirks.

"What do you mean, no?"

I shake my head and ball up my fists. This brat is messing
with me!

"That's not what you were going to say!"

"How do you know? Can you read my thoughts?"

I open my mouth, then clamp it shut. He chuckles, the
jerk.

"Tell me," I say, crossing my arms.

Thorne runs his palm over his face.

"It was a thought that I had no right to say out loud."

"Why?"

"Because it was an intense thought. It was… a promising thought. One I shouldn't have as your head of security."

"I swear to all the gods of the world you better tell me, Thorne Bartholomew DuPont."

I've lost the conviction in my words, especially using Thorne's middle name, which he'd reluctantly told me when I got bored during the ride to one of my meetings and wanted to know more about his life. I barely got the name out of him before he shut down sharing time when Millie called me.

Thorne shakes his head, amused. I think he enjoys me being bossy. Or maybe he likes disobeying orders and being a brat.

Would Thorne let me tie him up and spank that bubble butt of his—

"Layla," Thorne groans.

Right. I've turned myself on and by the look at the tent in his pants, he can smell just how wet I am right now.

"Please."

I don't know why I'm getting so emotional over this or why I need his validation so badly. He must have heard the desperation in my voice because his teasing demeanor falls, and he sighs.

"When you laugh, it's as if the sun rises without turning me to stone. It's warm, beautiful, and I want to bask in it."

I swallow as pressure builds behind my eyes.

Fuck, I'm going to cry. I *hate* crying.

Thorne unbuckles his seatbelt and slides over to me.

"Hey. I'm sorry, I didn't mean to upset you. Please don't cry."

"I'm not crying," I sob.

Goddamn it. Bloody tears are not sexy. I should be mad at Thorne for making me cry but how can I? No one has ever said such beautiful words to me.

Thorne cups my face, wiping a bloody tear off my cheek with his thumb. He sticks the thick digit in his mouth to lick it clean.

His eyes widen and he stills—like stone—as if contemplating his next move. I know exactly what he wants to do. He just needs my permission.

"Do it," I say, lust taking control of my voice.

He doesn't hesitate and leans forward, flattening his tongue against my cheek and running it up to lick away the bloody streak left by my tears.

I close my eyes as lust washes over my body. Thorne, still cupping my face in his hands, switches to the other side, and once the streaks are gone, I expect him to pull away.

He doesn't. He kisses me instead.

It's as if fireworks have been set off inside me, bright bursts of light fill my vision and my body shakes.

Did... did a kiss just make me come?

My body's reaction seems to fuel Thorne on, and he slides his tongue past my lips to massage my own. I moan and squirm and grip his shirt to pull him closer. Blood fills my mouth, and I'm not sure if it's mine or his since both of our fangs are out and this kiss is anything but gentle.

One of his hands skims down my front and behind the band of my pants. His tail wraps around my leg, pulling it open and without ending our kiss, he sinks one of his thick fingers inside me.

I arch my back, and he swallows my moan as he pumps in and out, matching our frantic kiss. My walls close around him but that doesn't slow him down.

Thorne's kisses move down across my jaw and to my neck where he scrapes his fangs across my skin.

"Yes, please."

"Please, what, Layla? Tell me," he murmurs and sucks on a spot hard enough that if I were human, it'd leave a hickey.

"Bite me, please."

And he does.

When his fangs sink into my neck, he thrusts his finger into me one final time, curling the tip to hit that special spot.

I erupt with an orgasm.

My walls clamp down on his finger and my entire body shakes. Thorne moans into my neck as he drinks my blood like a man dying of thirst.

When he unlatches himself, he leans his forehead against mine, breathing as if he's just flown around the world. I place my palm over his chest, loving the feel of his thudding heart.

"I've never came like that before," he says. "All I did was fuck you with my finger and drink your blood."

He sits up and glances down at the wet spot on the crotch of his pants.

A knock on my window causes me to jump. That's when I realize we've stopped. We're at our destination.

I burst out laughing.

"What?"

"The driver," I say, consumed with giggles.

Thorne's eyes widen, then he smiles and laughs with me.

I just let Thorne finger fuck me and drink my blood in the back of this town car... with no privacy divider... for the driver to see everything.

Now the young vampire stands outside my window, waiting for us to leave the car. A pained look is plastered on his face, his hands clasped in front of his groin.

I need to distract Thorne before he notices the driver's erection, clearly turned on by what he unwillingly witnessed.

"I'm going to need to go to the bathroom and fix myself before we head into the meeting," I say, opening the door.

"Same. Except, I don't think I'll get this jizz stain out of my pants. Every supe in the room will be able to smell us."

"Good. Let them." I smirk and wink at Thorne over my shoulder as we enter WOVE headquarters.

Chapter 8 - Vara

Well isn't this interesting?

Layla and Thorne walk in looking thoroughly fucked. They attempted to clean up beforehand, but I can smell her all over him. It's also hard to miss the wet stain on the front of his pants.

Did he really think water could hide his cum?

I'm not jealous, but I am annoyed that I didn't get to take part.

Layla's lips are still slightly puffy from Thorne's kisses and two pink dots peek out over the collar of her blouse.

He *bit* her.

She's healed already but the marks have yet to fade entirely.

My tail whips back and forth, and I squeeze my thighs together, imagining how fucking sexy it must have been to see him drinking from her.

Layla takes her place at the front of the table, chatting with Korna—the fae representative chosen for the committee. He's flirting heavily, but Layla is too kind and either doesn't notice or she does and doesn't want to be rude. Thorne steps forward to interrupt the two when I stand and walk around the table's edge.

"Queen Aldana," I say, shoving my tall and thick body in front of Korna. He scoffs and sputters incoherent words before walking away and sitting in his seat at the table, scowling at me. "Fresh orgasms look quite lovely on you."

She narrows her eyes.

"Thank you. I had two of them."

Oh, I hadn't expected her to match my sass.

I glance over her shoulder at Thorne, standing off to the side. He's never too far, always within touching distance. He raises a brow then smiles, showing me his fangs.

Cocky brat.

"Don't think I've forgotten my promise. You will be fucked by the both of us. Instead of *two* orgasms, you'll get six."

I smirk when she sucks in a sharp breath. Vampires don't need to breathe, but it's a habit to keep their human appearance in front of mortals. So, to get that reaction from her is quite the feat.

"And it won't be just once. We're going to fuck you often. We'll have you begging for it… make that pretty little pussy and asshole hurt. And once Thorne fills you up with all his cum, I'll drink it out of you."

The room has gone quiet. Okay, maybe I went a little far with that last line. I mean, it's definitely going to happen, but I suppose the other supes in the room didn't need to hear it. I hope they're at least enjoying the show.

I expect Layla to shrink into herself with embarrassment. Instead, she leans in and says, "Don't threaten me with a good time."

"Do we all get to fuck the new vampire queen or just Vara and the gargoyle?" Johnathan, the werewolf representative, asks.

The beta for Big Apple werewolf pack stands just inside the conference room door, arms crossed over his expansive chest. He's got sandy blond hair and golden eyes to match his golden smile. He's a big guy all around and shorter than the average man.

"That's enough, John. Take your seat," Layla says, already annoyed with the mouthy were.

He's got a reputation for being a prankster and a gossiper.

Everyone already knows about the new vampire queen giving a show at the ball nearly a week ago. It was a celebration, and we weren't the only ones publicly fucking that night. No one batted an eye.

But supes might start talking if they know Layla is *still* fucking her guard and the only sphinx in New York City.

Possibly the world.

I frown at the thought of being the only one left.

"Take your seat as well, Vara." My heart flutters at her dismissive tone. I scorn myself for challenging her authority right now.

She's leading this new committee, and I just announced to the room that she's being fucked by one of its members and the supe hired to protect her.

I'm an asshole.

"The energy in the room is weird," Locheran says, walking through the door. He plops down in a chair next to me. "And it smells like sex in here."

Locheran sniffs towards Layla and Thorne. His eyes widen, then he wiggles his brows at them. They both ignore him.

I expected Thorne to represent the gargoyles on this committee, but it makes sense that it's Locheran. He's the commander for the gargoyle king's army so we'll need his expertise on potential battle plans. Thorne's only job is to protect Layla and lead her security team. He can't have any distractions.

Layla herself is a beautiful distraction that he's clearly failed to avoid.

"Vara, you're looking extra bitchy today," Locheran says, smiling.

He's always been a beautiful beast. He's got muscles for days—as most gargoyles do. He's around my height. His hair is navy blue—lighter compared to the king's midnight blue that almost appears black—and Locheran's skin is a darker shade of purple.

He's cocky as hell and women these days would call him a fuck boy.

"Only because you're here... sitting next to me. Annoying me," I say.

"It's an honor." He salutes me, then tosses up his middle finger, which doesn't have the effect he thinks it does since he only has four fingers.

"Clearly, this committee is made up of children," Layla mumbles.

More supernatural representatives enter the room including a wolf shifter, a spirit, a demon, a centaur, a mothman, an orc, Gorgan the dragon in his human form—to name a few.

No angel rep, not that I'm surprised.

Once everyone's settled, and the monsters who can't physically be here have joined via video conference, Layla begins.

"Thank you all for taking part in this ambitious plan."

My heart beats a little faster seeing her so regal before us. Millie was a great queen, but I know she didn't want the role. Layla, however, was born to lead.

"I want to begin with a few rules," Layla continues. "First and foremost, it's imperative that only the beings on this committee keep the details of what we discuss, and the plan we construct, confidential. The only exceptions are your superiors or the elders who already know about the unveiling."

There's some mumbling of agreement but everyone nods.

"Second, I want everyone to be vocal. Any doubts you might have, let them be known. We cannot have a half-ass plan. And third, please be civil. We won't agree on every-thing, but we *must* compromise. That's the only way this will work."

More mumbles of agreement.

"Okay. I'd like to start with the first step: befriend-ing high-profile humans. Politicians, celebrities, athletes, CEOs, social media influencers. Anyone we can form a trusting relationship with who has power and sway.

"I will be attending several events over the next few months: parties, fundraisers, sporting events. Whatever it takes. Any human passing supe, or one who has the ability to mask, is highly encouraged to accompany me or attend events of your own.

"As for roles..."

Layla looks at me.

"Vara will be the ambassador between humans and supernaturals. Basically, PR before, during, and after our reveal. Locheran and the gargoyles will be in charge of a battle plan in case this all goes to hell. The witches," Layla continues, nodding to Myla who is one of the most powerful witches in our area aside from the coven leader, "will be there to cast protection spells or intervene with magic, whatever the case may be. To be honest, I have no idea what to expect. I could see it going three ways: the majority of humans accept us, only half are on board, or they all revolt and capture us to experiment on us."

"Gods," Korna mumbles.

Layla sighs. "I won't sugarcoat this. We all know the risks. We have to be prepared for everything."

She crosses her arms, a stern look on her face. She's so beautiful and confident in this moment. She's commanding all our attention like a siren of the night.

"I will be clear... compulsion will not be allowed. We will not mind control humans in any way to accept our existence. We will not threaten or bribe."

The committee members all nod their understanding.

"Good. Now..." She starts up a computer and opens the PowerPoint program. She scrunches her nose at the blank screen, then proceeds to tap the mouse and press buttons. A young vampire—one turned within the last decade—eventually joins her to troubleshoot the issue. She smiles at him, and he gives her a fanged grin back—he'd be blushing if he wasn't dead because that's what Layla does to those in her presence. The young vamp returns to his spot along the back wall next to Thorne who scowls at him. "This plan will take input from all of you. All ideas are welcome. Again, we have just under eight months to form this plan before presenting it at the International Supernatural Conference held here in New York City. As we move forward, I'm sure we'll need to assign more roles. I believe we'll need someone in charge of technology. I suspect once we show ourselves to the world, fake and manipulated videos will be posted online to implicate us as evil. Those videos along with any showing alleged supernatural attacks must be promptly taken down."

The griffin rep raises his hand.

"Yes, Bowden?"

"I'm good at that shit, I'll volunteer for tech."

"Wonderful." Layla beams at the winged creature. "I'm sure you'll be useful in launching the production unit that will broadcast informational videos Vara will star in."

"Naturally," Locheran snorts, and I slap my knuckles on his arm.

Layla clicks the computer's mouse and the screen changes. It's a silly graphic with cartoon monsters hugging.

"Unity. It's not something we have amongst species. We have parties and we fuck around with each other, but that's the extent of our collaborations. Aside from the gargoyles who often entrust us to help when evil is threatening our world."

We just don't trust each other. We're all power-hungry alphas who don't do well with authority.

"That needs to change," Layla continues. "It's imperative that we learn to live amongst ourselves before we can come out of the shadows. I recommend you all consider planning more interspecies parties over the next few months. *Not* sex parties. Get creative. Have a movie night. Or go bowling together—I don't care. Make friendships and form allies. I fear we will need them if this plan works."

Layla clicks again, showing a slide with a conference table and a smiling and waving vampire... who looks a lot like her. She definitely picked out the graphics for this PowerPoint presentation.

Fuck, she's adorable.

"Committee meetings. I think we can start off with twice a month and as the months go by, if we decide we need more meetings, we'll adjust accordingly."

Korna raises his hand, and Layla calls on him.

"How long will these meetings last?"

Layla shrugs. "An hour. Two? However long we need to make progress."

She ends the presentation with a slide that has her contact info, including email and phone number.

"I think we have a lot to consider so I will end things here. Bring ideas to the table for the next meeting. If you have any questions or concerns, please text or email me."

The meeting only lasted about fifteen minutes when Layla dismisses us. A few supes crowd her, speaking enthusiastically. The tension rolling off Thorne is palpable. He clearly doesn't like them being that close to her.

After thirty minutes of conversations, the last supe exits the room. I stand and smooth my hand down my stomach, shuttering my wings. Layla watches the movements and looks away when her fangs drop. I'm about to scold her when Thorne grabs her by the chin and moves her head back to me.

"No hiding your *lust*, Layla," he says, his deep voice reverberating throughout my body.

She lifts her head and straightens her shoulders.

"There's our queen," I say.

I stalk toward her, her eyes turning black and her nipples hardening through the thin fabric of her top, letting me know she's braless. I palm her cheek, and she briefly closes her eyes before opening them half-hooded.

"I am dying for us to take you home so we can give you all the orgasms I promised," I begin.

Layla frowns. "But?"

"But I own too many nightclubs, and I've already missed ten calls from many of them tonight. I'm working on a temporary replacement so I can put more focus on this committee... on you and Thorne, but they won't be ready to take over for at least another two weeks."

Layla's frown deepens, and I stifle the urge to kiss between her furrowed brows. I smirk and place a gentle kiss on her lips instead.

"Patience, my needy Layla-pop."

Thorne is behind Layla, and he snakes his hands around her waist. She leans into him, giving him access to her neck. He scrapes his fangs over the lush skin.

"How did she taste?" I ask.

He latches his palm onto the nape of my neck.

"Like a dream," he says and covers my mouth with his.

The kiss is surprisingly gentle, and I moan against his lips, allowing his tongue to slip in. I gasp when I can still taste Layla's blood.

How fascinating.

When Thorne releases me from the kiss, he turns to let Layla taste *me* on his lips. I can smell how wet she is for us already, and I groan, desperate to take care of her. But I can't neglect my clubs that I worked so hard to own.

"Two weeks, my dear." I turn to Thorne. "Tease her. Give her a taste, but wait for me, yes?"

He nods, the corner of his mouth tilting up. Perhaps already thinking about all the ways to get our vampire babe hot and bothered.

Chapter 9 - Thorne

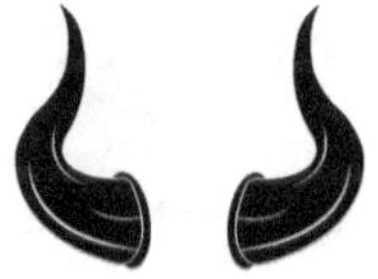

Torture.

It's the only way I can describe the past two weeks.

I kept my promise to Vara, despite how badly I wanted to sink my cock inside Layla's sweet cunt.

That's not saying that we haven't fooled around.

I've pleasured her with my fingers and feasted on her pussy while her legs were wrapped tightly around my head. I drank her pleasure after she came. She's also sucked me off a few times, mostly while in the car on our way to a meeting or an event.

I've never been so... feverish for another being. My need to be near her is nearly suffocating.

I can't understand it, and I've stopped fighting it. I may have said it was a bad idea to get involved with Layla, but it's never felt so *good*. So *right*.

I've talked to Xander about my feelings for the vampire and the sphinx, though we haven't seen her since the first meeting of SUC—I chuckle at the acronym, still funny several weeks later. Xander has experienced the emotions of a mate, and he agrees that I'm going through something similar. There's a tugging in my chest when Layla or Vara are not in my presence. It's not painful, but it's constant, as if my heart is attempting to leave my chest in search of them. Overwhelming desire fills my body when I lay eyes on them. There's also the unexplainable need to protect Layla and the jealousy when another being smiles at her or places a hand on her arm or shoulder.

I assume those same protective and jealous feelings are there for Vara as well.

Xander was thrilled for me until realizing I'm experiencing all this for *two* women. He's been alive for a lot longer than me, and he's never heard of a supernatural being having two mates. Though he said it's not impossible.

Nothing is impossible when it comes to supernaturals.

I've yet to bring it up with either woman, mostly because they've both been too busy. This isn't the kind of discussion to have in passing.

"You're being extra broody tonight," Layla says with a sigh, though I don't miss the humor in her voice. "Perhaps if I rode your cock, that would make you smile."

She giggles when I do, in fact, smile.

"I knew it. Look..." She scoots over to me, and her hand falls to my groin. She rubs her palm over my hardening cock. "I know Vara wanted us to wait for her, but what if we have a quickie? Surely, that wouldn't count."

We're in an SUV, heading to the second meeting of the Supernatural Unveiling Committee. After the show we put on during the drive the first time, we've made sure to change her transportation for one that included a privacy divider, which is currently up.

Her hand slips behind the band of my pants, and she wraps her short fingers around my bulbous base. I take Layla by the throat and her fangs drop immediately.

"Patience, Bunny."

She snarls at the nickname, still not a fan.

I'm not an adorable animal. Bunnies are prey. I'm a predator, she had said the first time I called her bunny. She then proceeded to scrunch her adorable button nose, like a bunny.

I moan when she tightens her grip and fists up and down the length until I leak precum from the tip. She uses it for lube and speeds up while her free hand roughly massages my balls through my pants.

Just how I like it.

I loosen my grip around her neck and extract my claws, letting one of them slice the side of her throat. Leaning over, I use my long tongue to lick up the blood beading out of the cut. She groans the same time I do.

"You're close," she mumbles through her desire.

She must feel my balls clenching.

"I want you to come down my throat."

I release her neck, and she takes my cock completely out of my pants. The moment her soft, plush lips wrap around the tip, I erupt.

I buck up into her mouth, my entire cock sliding in until the tip hits the back of her throat. I hold her head there while I release jets of my seed that she swallows greedily as if she's been dying of thirst.

"Fuck, Layla," I moan.

I remove my cock from her mouth, and she licks her lips, humming.

"Let me take care of you now," I say, moving to cup her pussy.

She pushes my hand away and points out the window.

"We're here, but don't worry. That felt so good for me too."

She pats my cheek and a second later, one of the security team members who followed us in another SUV opens her door.

Most everyone has arrived when we enter the meeting room. Vara is sitting on the table at Layla's seat, chatting with Brian, the shifter rep. Vara immediately ends their conversation and stands, pushing the shifter to the side.

I chuckle, not even surprised by the dismissive move. Brian rolls his eyes and takes his seat.

"Lollipop," she purrs, taking Layla's hands in hers. Vara leans in, giving Layla a kiss on each cheek. "You look lovely. That outfit fits you like a second skin."

It's true. Layla is wearing a dark green wrap dress that hugs her thick frame deliciously.

"It will look even better on my floor," Vara whispers, though whispering around supernaturals is pointless. Everyone heard the sphinx proposition the vampire.

It's fine. They all know something is going on between us. Especially with me and Layla since we always walk in smelling like sex.

Layla blanches. "That's a terrible line, V."

Vara chuckles, amused at the shortening of her name. She shrugs. "Terrible but true."

The sphinx walks around Layla, placing her hand on her shoulder.

"I hope this meeting is quick. I have plans for you."

She turns to me.

"And you."

With a wink, Vara takes her seat.

I cover my groin, the thoughts of tonight finally happening have my cock hard despite Layla draining it minutes earlier. It desperately wants to knot inside a warm pussy.

Or asshole.

We're not picky.

The first time I had that thought, it surprised me. I never had an overwhelming need to knot inside any of my previous partners. Most of the time, knotting is intended for mating... but it doesn't have to be. It can knot for my partner's pleasure.

I lock eyes with Vara, and she lifts a perfect brow at me. I must not be hiding my arousal well. My phone buzzes in my pants pocket, and I pull it out to see a text from Locheran.

Hey Mister Growlypants, keep it down over there.

Loch

Fuck! I growled again?

I reply with a middle finger emoji and tuck my phone away.

I let my thoughts consume me as Layla leads the meeting. She's so regal up there, powerful, inspiring. She answers questions and concerns from the group the best that she can. To be honest, we won't know if any of this planning will be helpful. We have no idea how the humans will react.

Locheran will have the biggest job of preparing security measures, not just locally, but ones that can be utilized around the world. He'll also need to come up with a war plan in case that's the outcome of the unveiling.

Layla discusses some of the human events she'll be attending over the next few months and asks for volunteers to attend with her. The witch, werewolf, shifter, and fae reps all agree to attend at least one of them.

The idea is that once a supe has made a strong enough connection with a human, and once they trust them enough, they'll reveal their true forms. The human's reaction will be gauged and if it goes badly, a witch or vampire will be on standby to help.

Layla doesn't want to implement compulsion to sway acceptance, but it might be needed to avoid problems with a human that could put our lives at risk.

For the most part, Layla is confident that most mortals we befriend will be accepting. She wants to have a big group of well-known humans at the convention taking place in about seven months. That way we can show the supernatural committee it's possible for humans to accept us.

Vara already has connections with a few human journalists, and she plans to attend upcoming journalism conferences to do more networking. She said we'll want to have interviews lined up on network news shows, with newspapers and online blogs, etc. She also wants to reach out to some influencers. There are a few supernatural ones who have accounts appearing as cosplayers but what people believe are costumes or makeup are actually their true forms. It's something the elders are not fans of but trying to convince younger supes to stay off social media is like speaking to the wind.

After an hour of discussions, Layla finally ends the meeting. Vara stands as the last person exits and joins Layla at the front of the table. I step forward too on Layla's other side.

"I'm so proud of you, Lollipop." Vara traces her fingertips up and down Layla's arm. "So commanding up there. Do you like to be in control?"

Layla nods then frowns.

"Yes, but only because I don't like being controlled. When I was human, my husband was abusive. After I killed him during my turn, I staked my sire, who was just as bad, I vowed to never let another man control me. In the bedroom, I tend to have the same attitude but…"

"But…"

Layla smiles shyly. I rarely see her shy around others. It's mostly in private where her vulnerability tends to come out.

"I like when you control me, V."

"You like taking orders from me?"

Layla nods.

Vara shifts her golden eyes to me.

"What about Thorne? Do you want him to control you? Give you orders? Or do you want him to get down on his knees before you?"

Layla sucks in a sharp breath, her eyes darkening as lust takes over.

"I want him on his knees."

My cock jumps at her words.

"Good girl," Vara whispers, taking Layla's chin so she can kiss her. It's a quick, but passionate kiss. "Not here though. My place isn't far."

Vara nods to me, and I open the door. She takes Layla's hand and leads her out of the room while I fall behind, Layla's other hand in mine.

Layla's security team escorts us out of the building to a row of SUVs waiting at the curb. The guards split between the first and last vehicle while Layla, Vara, and I pile in the middle one.

The drive lasts ten minutes before we're pulling into a parking garage underneath a high-rise in Lower Manhattan. The building is sleek and modern despite the surrounding architecture that's hundreds of years old.

We pass a security booth manned by two men, one human and the other a bear shifter. They nod to Vara, somewhat nervously, which doesn't surprise me being how intimidating she can appear. I can't imagine how powerful she must look in her human form. The two smile at Layla next and it's not a friendly smile. It's full of dangerous want, predator leering—a reaction she gets a lot from men because Layla is beautiful and voluptuous with thick thighs, a plump and biteable ass, and tits that perfectly fit in my hands.

Mine.

The men's eyes widen when they spot me, realizing their mistake of looking at my woman.

"I'm yours, Thorne," Layla whispers and squeezes my hand.

Did she know I was seconds from gouging their eyes out?

She brings my hand up to her mouth and kisses my knuckles. My tense body relaxes immediately.

"Don't worry, they'll be taken care of by the morning," Vara says.

She could mean firing them or killing them, but neither of us ask her to clarify.

Vara's building is almost as secure as Layla's as we approach a private elevator. Of course Vara would have her own entrance. She taps an access card to the reader and the doors open. She taps the card again and the car rises. It takes about a minute before we arrive at the penthouse, some sixty floors up.

The doors open to a gallery foyer with several large closets, a half bath, and a laundry room.

We walk on, entering an open room with vaulted ceilings that have to be at least twenty feet tall with floor-to-ceiling windows. I don't doubt they stay open to let the sun stream in during the day. Sphinxes love the sun—which makes me wonder why Vara tends to live a nocturnal lifestyle.

I see she has UV protectors on the windows. Has she always had them, or did she install them recently after meeting two supernaturals who can't walk in the sun?

She gives us a quick tour. The living space has a gas fireplace, a huge television hangs over it, taking up a good chunk of wall. There's an open dining area and a kitchen any chef would salivate over. Aside from the stainless-steel appliances, there's a huge island topped with marble and seating for four.

"These floors are beautiful," Layla gasps.

"Brazilian walnut," Vara responds as if expecting Layla to know what that means. When the vampire queen 'oos,' I realize Brazilian walnut flooring must be something luxurious.

The penthouse's main level has two bedrooms and a media room. Vara keeps it full of art, record albums, and musical instruments. I assume she can play all of them: guitar, piano, cello, violin.

As immortals, life can become boring when there's nothing new left to experience. Many of us learn all the languages and teach ourselves how to play every instrument imaginable. Like myself. I can play several, including the piano and guitar.

Vara points upstairs to a loft, explaining that's where the main bedroom is located. But instead of taking us up there, we go outside to a private wraparound terrace with lush landscaping, a fire pit, a built-in hot tub, grilling station, and amazing views of the city.

"Vara," Layla sighs. "This is just magnificent. I love my penthouse in Midtown, but the views in Lower Manhattan are unmatched."

One World Trade Center towers over us and off in the distance, the Empire State Building shines bright in pink and blue. The air is fresh and clear up this high, and it reminds me how much I miss flying and stretching my wings. I don't fly nearly as much as I used to. Most of my patrols to protect this city are stationary or on the ground.

Vara smiles at the compliment, but it doesn't reach her eyes. I can't imagine how hard she must have worked and all the sacrifices she's made throughout her life to get to this point.

"Would you all like something to drink?"

Vara waves us back inside and into the kitchen. She grabs a glass of wine for herself, and I ask for water. Layla also takes wine, but I have to wonder if she needs blood.

When was her last feed?

Should we call for a donor? Can she have my blood?

I guess I don't know much about vampires. We help them when needed, like tracking down rogue vampires, but until I became Layla's head of security, I had never personally known a vampire. I never sat down and chatted with one.

Surprisingly, I've never fucked one either.

I suppose if Layla needed blood, she'd have already taken care of it. I do know that vamps have synthetic blood they can drink to hold them over until they can get a donor.

I would let Layla drink from me.

The thought of Layla sinking her teeth into my neck sends a wave of lust down my spine and around to my cock. If it's anything like when I fed from her, then yes, I'd very much like Layla to bite me.

"Are you okay?" Layla asks as Vara sets a glass of water in front of me. "What are you thinking about that has your heart racing?"

"He wants you to bite him," Vara says with a chuckle.

"What? How do you even know that?" I stumble over my words, but don't deny Vara's accusation. I glance at Layla, and she winces.

"You do kinda look like you want me to bite you. Your pupils have expanded so much that I can't even see the blue in your eyes anymore. Your fangs have also dropped, and you're drooling."

I wipe the back of my hand against my mouth, but it comes back dry. Layla giggles.

She's teasing me?

I smile at her adorable humor. She rarely shows it. She hasn't had time to be so carefree in this new role of hers.

I also find myself smiling a lot more since meeting these women.

Instead of answering me, Vara takes a sip of her wine.

"I have a theory. One I assume you both have as well," she says, swishing the liquid in her glass. She takes another drink, torturing us a little by dramatically drawing out her thoughts. I'm ready to strangle her, then immediately get turned on by the idea, when Vara finally says, "I believe we are mates."

Layla and I say nothing for several seconds.

"Who? You and Layla?" I ask.

"Me and Thorne?" Layla offers.

"You and me?" I add.

Vara rolls her eyes, clearly hearing the panic in our voices. "All of us. All *three* of us."

"Are you... um... all... the three of us?" Layla says, words failing her. In the short time I've known the vampire queen, I know she's rarely left speechless.

"Mates. We're mates," Vara repeats, exasperated by our overreaction.

"Oh," I mumble because somehow, I've also forgotten how words work.

I was *just* thinking about mates earlier. So, I'm not crazy? If Vara is validating my suspicions, perhaps it really is true.

"But... it's... absurd," Layla says. She throws up both of her arms in frustration, her voice a pitch higher. The corner of my mouth tilts up at how adorable she looks while having an existential crisis. "Blood mates for vampires are rare. I mean, sure, Millie found hers, but she's only one of three known cases. So for me to have found not one but two? It's unheard of."

"But not impossible," Vara counters.

Layla's face twists as she lets herself process the information. She frowns; her brows furrow. Then one brow lifts as a part of herself considers the possibility.

"I mean... I did have this thought at one point and it would explain... a lot of things," Layla says. "Like why I'm so fucking horny around you two. But I dismissed the idea of us all being mates because there's not a known case of it happening."

Vara turns to me. "What do you believe?"

I shake my head. "Mates do not come easily for my kind either. Xander didn't find his until his 999th year of living. Gargoyles are cursed beings just like vampires."

How strange to think I might have actually found my fated mate... no, *mates*. While it's imperative for royals to find theirs before their 1000th birthday, otherwise they permanently turn to stone, it's somewhat rare for all other gargoyles. Or rather, it takes centuries for us to find them. Even my friend Locheran has yet to find his, and he's about to turn 1,000.

I would consider myself lucky to have found mine at age 712.

"Cursed to the night, yes," Vara muses. "Cursed to never fall in love? That you are inherently evil? No. The witches may be petty cunts. Passionate lovers too…"

Vara's words trail off, and her cheeks redden as she bites her lip, probably thinking about a past lover who was a witch. I have to agree with her there. Witches are fantastic lovers. The magic they exude, especially during sex and when they come, is transcending.

"What I'm trying to say is a witch's curse can weaken if the sole belief behind the magic has proven to be false in nature. Things you once believed to be true can change and that includes the idea behind mates."

"But how do you know for sure?" Layla asks, crossing her arms and shifting on her feet.

Vara sighs, taking a sip of her wine as she gathers her words. "To be honest, I felt you both the moment you were born. Thorne, your birthday is June 1st, correct? You're 712 years old?"

I let out a long stream of air and nod.

"I remember that day. It was as if a part of me had… woken, and I could breathe a little easier. Nothing sexual, of course, just… freeing. Then a second shift happened about three years later on March 24th. Another part of myself opened. I'm guessing that was when you were born, Layla."

Layla slowly nods; her mouth open in awe as she intently listens to Vara.

"I hadn't thought much of these feelings, mostly because I didn't understand what they meant at the time. I went on with my life. I had long left Egypt and traveled around the world. I drowned my loneliness and depressive thoughts with extravagant things. A life of luxury. Plenty of sex. Except the one thing I always wanted failed me: I never loved.

"I was in Europe in the 1930s when hunters found me, so I flew across the ocean to the Americas, landing in New York City. I had sensed you both nearly immediately. You were both here in the 30s, correct?"

"I got here in 1921," Layla says.

"1922," I add.

I also remember the night I arrived in New York City. I'd flown across the Atlantic Ocean after accepting Xander's invitation to join his army. I was excited, eager. I couldn't explain why though.

Now it's making more sense. Layla was here. *My mate.*

I can't believe our paths never crossed in all this time. Though, I took my new position with Xander's army seriously. I didn't socialize outside of my fellow gargoyle soldiers. Not until recently when Locheran started dragging me to human clubs to be his wingman.

I'd heard of Layla, of course. She was the vampire queen's royal advisor. I'd also heard about Vara. The arrival of the sphinx, who is likely one of the last of her kind, was all supes could talk about for months. For me, the night of her arrival left me in pain, my chest aching. It lessened as the years went by, but never fully leaving my body. Now I know that the constant pull was my heart calling out for my mates.

It took way too long to find them too.

"Instead of seeking either of you out," Vara continues, "I decided to let destiny take the lead. I let fate bring you both to me."

I rub my palm down my face. "Okay... but why are we just now finding each other? And why both of us?"

"I'm not sure," Vara says. "But if it's to protect each other, then I will lay down my life for you both. If it's to fight for our kind together when we're revealed to the humans, then I will battle until my final heartbeat. If it's to... give you all the pleasures of the world, then I will gladly grab Layla by the hips and bury my face in her delectable cunt while you take me from behind, Thorne."

Fuck.

My cock twitches at the words.

Both women jerk their heads to me, clearly feeling my lust.

"No fucking way," Layla says, breathless. "I thought I was losing my mind. Anytime Thorne seemed to be turned on, I was too. Our orgasms when fooling around have been nothing short of intense... but now it all makes sense."

"Shared pleasure," I say in awe.

"It appears so," Vara says, walking to where Layla and I stand at the kitchen island. "I felt it every time you and Thorne were together without me."

She places her palm on my chest and smooths it over my pec, then down my stomach, her claws getting dangerously close to my cock. Her touch burns my skin despite the fabric of my shirt between us.

"If we truly are mates," Vara continues, "then we will be able to hear each other's thoughts. That's how I knew you wanted Layla to bite you."

I glance at Layla, and her fangs are bared.

"You thought the words 'bite me' and while they were quiet and weak in my head, it was very clearly your voice. I believe after we complete the bond, the shared thoughts will become more frequent, stronger. However, like other fated mate couples, we'll learn to control what we want to hear and what we send out."

"Complete the bond…" Layla says the words dreamily, and I can't help but picture all three of us tangled together in the throes of hot fingers-and-tails-and-my cock knotted in a cunt-sex.

The women both whimper, me unintentionally sending a shot of lust their way.

"Yes," Vara says breathlessly. "But here's the problem."

My body tenses, waiting for her to give us the bad news. Because if it sounds too good, it must be. There will always be a 'but.'

"I have no idea how a bond between three mates is completed or what will happen after."

Chapter 10 - Vara

"**Y**ou're not sure how to complete the bond?" Thorne asks, shifting on his feet.

"In theory I do. Certainly, it can't be too different from how vampires and gargoyles complete their bonds." I wave my hand at Layla then Thorne.

Layla perks up, seeming to catch on. "You think we should fuck and bite each other during simultaneous orgasms until the bond clicks into place so to speak?"

Thorne's already dark purple face deepens with a blush. He smiles too. It's strange to see the emotion on the broody gargoyle. He's all hard lines and massive muscles yet the thought of being together with me and Layla transforms that intimidating exterior to a beautifully welcoming presence.

I bet he's really good at hugs.

I startle at the thought. I've never been one to give, or want, hugs. Touching in general is reserved for sexual pleasures. But to be hugged by either of these two... to be cuddled up in bed after multiple mind-blowing orgasms warms my entire body with something I've never felt: contentment.

I shrug. "We could, but the part I'm unsure of is how long the bonding stage will be afterwards. It could be anywhere from a few days or weeks to months."

Thorne's smile slowly fades.

"Right. While I would love nothing more than to have my cock and tail buried deep inside the both of you, and lose ourselves to the bond, Layla is the new vampire queen. She's booked for the next several months with meetings and appearances."

Layla scrunches her nose. "Unfortunately, he's right. I'm supposed to start making friends with human activists and political figures. I'll be attending charity events and community outreach programs. Anything to get my face on the local news to become well known to the humans. Same with Vara."

We stand in silence as we let our situation sink in.

"If I am Layla's mate," Thorne begins, "then I need to step down from my position, something I should have done the moment I suspected it. There are already rules in place for such things."

"There *are* rules," I say. "But I think you were chosen for this role for a reason, and if you are her mate, that means you will protect her at all costs. Anyone else could leave her vulnerable."

"Not if one of Xander's other soldiers takes my place."

"Thorne," I sigh. "Now isn't the time to follow rules. Loosen up for fuck's sake. We don't even know how the three-way bond works entirely. You shouldn't worry until it locks into place. Also, we probably shouldn't tell anyone of this. Multiple mates at the same time is unheard of. Supes are jealous creatures. They could attempt to break us apart, or worse, use us against Layla in her new position."

Thorne grimaces. "I already mentioned my... um... feelings for the both of you to Xander."

"And I talked to Millie too."

Of course. They have friends who they talk with about this kind of stuff. I wave my hand. "Fine, tell those you trust, but no one else. I'd like to keep this to ourselves as long as possible. I know it will come out eventually. It's inevitable. We just need more time to process what's happening between the three of us."

"So we really are mates?" Layla asks, awe and excitement filling her voice.

Thorne's wings flutter. I've noticed he does that a lot when he's delighted… or turned on. My eyes travel down his body to his bulge. He's *definitely* turned on.

"It's all happening so fast," Layla continues.

"Yes. It is," I say. "But like I said, by not completing the bond right away, it will allow our feelings to catch up to this intense attraction we're feeling toward each other."

That could also bite us in the ass. If we truly are mates, the bond will do everything in its power to bring us together. Everything will be amplified: our sexual need for one another, our protectiveness, the painful tug in our chest when we're apart…

Supernaturals are far more open to accepting a fated mate bond than a human. Most of us wait our entire lives to find the one who claims our heart. But our case is different. Our hearts are being shared and it's all too overwhelming, even for a supernatural. Not to mention that we have lived hundreds of years alone, not needing to depend on another.

Besides, a fated mate bond can be rejected. We still have a choice. Our bodies will only allow the bond to take hold if the other—or others—truly want it.

"I mean…" Layla says at the same time Thorne mumbles, "But…"

They're both pouting, and it's rather adorable.

"Oh no," I goad. "My poor horny *mates*."

Layla and Thorne stand on opposite sides of each other at the kitchen island, and I'm at the end between them. Extending my wings, I wrap the ends around them and drag them next to me.

Layla gasps at the unexpected move and Thorne humphs. I doubt the massive gargoyle has ever been manhandled before. He's strong, but so am I. I'd love nothing more than to toss him around. He's especially good at taking orders, pleasuring our queen at my words in the limo a few weeks ago. I'd love to sit back and tell him to touch and fuck Layla while I watch.

I lift my hands to cup their cheeks. "Who says we can't still fuck in the meantime?"

My tail moves between Layla's legs, and I skim the tip along her already soaked panties. She inhales a sharp breath when it pushes the material aside and brushes her slit.

"So wet for us, my darling."

I wrap my fingers around her throat and squeeze, pulling her close enough so I can cover her mouth with mine. The kiss is soft, sweet, but I'm hungry for more. I slip my tongue inside and lap up her honey taste. Her fangs have dropped, and they prick my lips, causing them to bleed.

Thorne's pleasure nips at my nerves. When I release Layla, I reach my hand up and close my fingers around the gargoyle's thick neck. It's harder to squeeze but with my supernatural strength, I manage enough to skirt that fine line of pain and pleasure.

I pull Thorne close to slant my mouth over his. His lips aren't as delicate as Layla's, but his kiss is just as sweet. Just as hungry. His tongue swipes over the cuts from Layla's fangs, and he groans at the taste of my blood.

It's as if it activates the animalistic parts inside him. He growls and bites down, his own fangs puncturing my lips. He sucks up the blood as it pours out, then he clasps my chin and turns my head so Layla can get her fill. The vampire's tongue lashes over my wound. It will start healing soon so she eagerly takes what she can.

She moans into my mouth as I move the hardened tip of my tail to her clit. It might not vibrate like a gargoyle's tail, but I still know how to work a clit.

I press down and massage the sensitive bud in quick circles, bringing Layla to the cusp of orgasm.

Thorne's fingers have found their way to my pussy, and he slides one in while Layla feeds off our bloody make out session.

There's a hand on my breast... large and calloused. Then another hand, soft and small, covers the other. Simultaneously, the vampire and gargoyle pinch and pull my nipples, causing me to scream out.

"Bedroom," I manage to moan.

I release their throats and Thorne removes his fingers, then slides them into Layla's mouth so she can lick off my pleasure.

Once his fingers are clean, I lead them up the stairs to my bedroom. I've kept the decor simple since I don't spend a lot of time up here. A few abstract paintings hang along the walls. The bedding on the king-sized mattress is white but the rest of the furniture around the room is black.

"In between us, Layla," I say and stand in front of her.

Thorne moves behind her and locks eyes with me. I nod, and his large hands move to her forearms. He smooths them up then around to her back where he takes hold of the zipper, slowly sliding it down.

Layla inhales sharply. I love how she lets us know just how much our touches affect her.

Thorne's hands slide underneath the fabric of the dress until it falls off her top half. I take over and peel it down her wide hips until it pools at her feet.

She steps out and while I'm kneeling before her, I help her out of her stilettos too.

"I rather like being on my knees before you, my queen," I say.

The words ignite her lust, and I lean into her pussy, running my nose up the center and inhaling.

"So fucking delectable."

I stand and begin undressing. Thorne follows my lead and when we're both as naked as Layla, we pause to take each other in.

Thorne is littered in scars, most across his chest and stomach, I assume from battles he's fought. His thick, tree-trunk thighs could crush melons, and his arms are riddled with muscles.

He's a warrior, through and through.

Thorne and I turn to Layla at the same time, and she takes a step back, her arms twitching as if she's thinking about covering herself.

"Don't you dare, Bunny," Thorne says, and I smirk. Such a good boy, scolding our mate. "We are about to worship every inch of this body. Why would you try to hide what is ours?"

He steps in front of her and sinks to his knees. He's tall enough for his head to line up with her tits. He leans forward and kisses between them.

"So perfect."

He moves his lips down to her stomach, kissing just above her belly button.

"So soft."

He takes hold of her hips and lifts her to put his mouth on her pussy. Extending his long, thick tongue, he licks up the slit before taking her clit in between his lips.

"So *ours*."

Layla moans, desperately holding onto his horns for leverage as Thorne thrusts his tongue in and out of her.

"Move her to the bed," I say, and he stands with Layla still on his tongue.

She squeezes his head between her legs as if fearing he'll drop her while he walks the few feet to the bed.

He lies down, spreading out his wings in anticipation of using them tonight. He adjusts Layla so she's in the perfect position above his face.

"Now ride his tongue, Layla."

Chapter 11 - Layla

Thorne's long, thick tongue pumps in and out of me. Tightly holding onto his horns, I match his thrusts, fucking him like Vara ordered me to.

"Don't hover. Smother him, my darling," Vara says, noticing me keeping my weight off Thorne's face.

Thorne's arms wrap around my thighs, holding me down. I worry he'll suffocate but maybe gargoyles are good at holding their breath. He doesn't seem worried and takes over, thrusting in and out of me at a speed I never knew a tongue could accomplish. A tongue that has expanded and is filling me to capacity.

He growls like a ravenous dog with a bone.

I feel Vara at my back. Her hands snake around my front to palm my breasts. She squeezes, then takes my nipples between her fingers. I cry out when she pinches and pulls. Thorne groans as my pussy walls close around his tongue.

"I'm close," I wheeze.

Vara's lips ghost across my neck as she continues to work my nipples. Thorne's nose grinds into my clit.

Fuck! That feels amazing.

"Come on his tongue, Layla. Show him how well he eats you out."

Thorne hums, the deep vibration buzzes against my clit. That's when I erupt with an orgasm, failing to hold in my scream.

"Such a good girl."

Vara moves away and cold air hits my back. I shiver and lift off Thorne's face. He pulls me down for a kiss and I whimper, tasting myself on his lips. He's a fantastic kisser. Soft and cautious yet consuming.

"On your back, Queen."

I don't hesitate to follow Vara's demands. Thorne moves out of the way so I can take his place on the bed.

"Thorne's going to fuck you while *I* ride *your* face.

I squeeze my thighs together, but Thorne pulls them back apart. He teases my soaked entrance with his thick fingers.

"So beautiful," he whispers.

"So *ours*," Vara responds.

I've been in a few threesomes over my time on this earth. Never have my lovers been so... possessive and attentive. They're putting my pleasure first, which I don't understand since we're all supposed to be mates.

I reach for Vara, and the sphinx mounts my face. At least with me, there's no chance I will die from suffocation. I skim my hands up her thighs, relishing the thin, silky layer of fur that lines most of her body.

Vara is a beautiful creature. I've thought so since the moment we met, even if I hid my feelings and stayed far away from her. Now I know why I had such an intense attraction to her. Though the fated mate bond allows us to have a choice, and it wouldn't have activated if I hadn't been attracted to her.

How could I not? She's tall, but not quite as tall as Thorne. Her gold fur fades at her shoulders when her human features take over. The golden feathers of her wings are so vibrant they almost sparkle. The clothes she wears do little to hide her perky breasts and delectable cunt. And she's so goddamn demanding. I typically like to be in control in the bedroom. Mostly because I never trusted my lover to take care of me and my needs. But I trust Vara. I trust Thorne. I will submit to them both and know they will never abuse their dominance.

Thorne spreads my legs wide enough to fit his big body in between. The tip of his bulbous cock presses at my slick opening as Vara settles on my face. My mouth covers her clit, and I suck and lash it with my tongue.

"Fuck!" she screams and bucks at the shot of pleasure.

Thorne continues to tease my pussy, sliding his cock up and down but refusing to put it inside me.

"Thorne," I mumble against Vara's clit. She hums at the zing of vibration.

"Tell me what you need, Bunny."

His deep voice washes over me, flooding my body with lust.

"I need you to fuck me. Now."

He doesn't give me warning, but I asked for it. He thrusts into me, and I cry out at the pain.

A good fucking pain as I adjust around his size.

Bloody tears fall down my cheeks and Vara swipes them with her finger before sucking it clean.

Lord that was hot.

I return to Vara's pussy, thrusting my tongue inside her as Thorne rails me with his massive cock.

It's too much.

My pleasure... Vara's... Thorne's.

My body shakes with an orgasm, and Thorne groans as my walls clamp around him. He doesn't stop and presses his finger to my clit, massaging it as he fucks me.

I hold onto Vara tightly, continuing to eat her out as her orgasm draws near. I slip my finger inside her asshole and pump slowly.

"I'm going to come," Vara says.

"Me too," I mumble, though the words aren't legible against Vara's clit.

When Thorne's cock starts vibrating, I fall apart.

We all do.

Simultaneously.

The room seems to shake, and my vision blurs.

I hear a thud, and a heavy body covers me seconds before I pass out.

When I wake, the sun has set, and Vara's UV shades are rising.

Wait.

I jolt upright and glance around the room.

Empty.

Did I... did I just have a sex dream about Thorne and Vara?

"You're awake," Thorne says, entering the room with a human behind him.

No. It was all too real.

"Oh. I... yes."

He waves to the petite redhead next to him.

"I brought you dinner."

I glance down at my body and realize someone has dressed me in pajamas: a light pink tank and matching shorts. They don't fit, and I'm stretching out the material so I'm assuming they're Vara's clothes, though I can't imagine her ever wearing these.

The human walks to the bed and sits down on the mattress next to me. She hands me her consent form that assures me she's here willingly and was not under the influence of compulsion upon signing it. The form is infused with magic so if the human lies, the ink will turn red.

She's eager. Her heart thunders in her chest, and she's wet with lust.

Many humans sign up to be donors because they find pleasure in pain. There are also fang bangers who seek out vampires to fuck while being fed from, nothing shameful about it, but we do step in if they become too forceful or needy and become addicted, which could make them ill from donating too much.

Thorne stands at the door, arms crossed, watching. I suddenly feel self-conscious about feeding in front of him, even though I feed in front of other vampires and supernatural beings all the time.

The human is shivering with anticipation, and my throat aches with hunger.

Fine. Guess I have an audience.

I angle my head and lock eyes with Thorne over her shoulder. He shifts on his feet as I extract my fangs. His pupils dilate, and he sucks in a breath when I sink them into the donor's neck. He steps forward but stops, realizing this isn't an invitation to join.

It takes only a few minutes for my thirst to be satisfied. I clean the donor's wound, and Thorne sends her away.

"There's a change of clothes on the dresser." He points to the stack. "I called your assistant, and she brought them over."

"What happened to us?" I ask, standing. I grab the clothes and head to the en suite bathroom. It's massive with a shower that could probably fit five people inside. There's a jacuzzi tub, a counter with three sinks—how convenient for three mates—and a separate room for the toilet.

"We all passed out," Thorne says, following me.

"Obviously, chatterbox." I roll my eyes, which causes the corner of Thorne's lip to turn up. "Care to elaborate?"

I set the black leggings, sports bra, and oversized sweater my assistant brought me on the counter. I could kiss her. Kenna is a human who knows about supernaturals because she's from Scotland where she grew up surrounded by lore. She's been with me for a decade now, so she probably knows me better than I know myself, including how I like to dress comfortably and crash on the couch to watch mindless television on these rare nights when I have no responsibilities.

Thorne leans his shoulder against the doorframe. He has no right to look that sexy. I trail my eyes down his body. He's wearing all black, like always. A short-sleeved shirt that stretches over his chest and black sweatpants that fail to hide the outline of his massive cock. His long black hair is up in a man bun and his wings are tucked to his back.

I want to run my fingers over the silky membrane. Would that turn him on? Would it make him moan?

Thorne clears his throat, his nostrils flaring.

Okay, this mate thing is exhausting. It's impractical to be horny this much.

"We're not really sure why it happened," Thorne says, ignoring my needy cunt. "Perhaps the shared pleasure was too overwhelming."

"Hmm. That would make sense."

To think... if we had exchanged blood, we might be bonded by now.

I know the bonding ritual is different for every couple—or throuple, in our case—depending on species and gender. For vampires, completing the bond entails ingesting each other's blood during sex and having mutual orgasms. Gargoyle bonding is similar except knotting is involved.

I squeeze my legs together at the thought of Thorne's knot filling me. He moves behind me and peels the silk pajama top off my body.

"I can undress myself." The words are husky as he removes the shorts next.

"Not when your thoughts are begging for pleasure," he says and places a kiss on my neck.

I stand on my tiptoes to curl my arm around his neck, which gives him better access to cup my pussy. It's still sore from the goddamn log Thorne carries around in his pants. Which surprises me since my vampire healing should have resolved the pain issue. Maybe that's part of the fated mate bond too. I don't know, but I don't necessarily hate having a reminder of how thoroughly I've been fucked.

"You heard my thoughts?"

"No," he says, huffing his hot breath against my skin. "But I can smell how turned on those naughty thoughts are making you. So insatiable."

He sinks a thick digit inside me.

"Fuck, Thorne," I groan.

He pumps in and out while his other hand squeezes my breast.

"You're already close, Bunny. This pussy is so needy. Come on my finger like a good girl."

God I love when he talks dirty to me, especially when he's a man of few words.

Thorne pinches my nipple and curls the tip of his finger, hitting that perfect spot.

I explode.

He removes his fingers and shoves them in my mouth. I whimper at my taste.

I turn and bury my hand down his pants to take hold of his cock. He sucks in a sharp breath when I wrap my cold fingers around him.

"Where's Vara?" I ask while pumping my fist up and down his length.

I expected her to have shown up by now.

"She said... she had some... business... to take care of. Fuck, Layla. You're really good at that."

With my other hand, I fondle Thorne's balls with a heavy grip, and he whimpers. He's always so vocal for us, and I can't get enough.

"Where do you want it?" I ask, feeling him close.

"Anywhere."

The second before he reaches his release, I kneel, and cum spurts all over my face. I open my mouth and stick out my tongue to catch some.

Once Thorne's drained, I hop in the shower to wash all of his cum off my face. I expected him to leave, but he stays, watching from the shower's doorway as I clean myself.

"Is Vara coming back soon?"

"I believe so."

I must be wrinkling my nose because Thorne leans in and boops it, not even caring that his arm gets wet.

"Bunny."

"I will bunny kick *you* if you do that again."

I stifle the urge to turn away from him to hide my amusement. Thorne notices and puffs his chest, proud of me for listening to him. I roll my eyes, which makes him smile.

This giddy feeling while around him... while around Vara... is so unusual. It reminds me of the time I had a crush on my neighbor when I was twelve years old. He was a year older than me, cute, and so sweet. I gushed about him to my sister any chance I got.

I want to scream to the world about my new mates.

Potential mates?

It's still so surreal.

Vampires are led to believe that we're cursed. We aren't meant to love. At least, that's what I believed, but Millie met her mate and now her heart beats again. Now she can tolerate the sun.

Will that happen for me? Will my heart start beating?

It aches in my chest as if preparing to do just that.

I return to the stream of water, grabbing Vara's body wash. I put the bottle's top to my nose and inhale. It smells like her.

Cherry blossoms.

"How long have you been awake?" I ask Thorne.

He's now propped himself against the shower's back wall, arms crossed. His tail whips back and forth, and he taps his fingers on his muscle-packed forearms.

It's as if he's battling with staying put or saying, 'fuck it' and joining me.

"About two hours."

"Did you dress me?"

"I did. I hope that was okay."

I step to him, and he tenses. I place my wet palms on his hard, shirt-covered chest and smooth them up and down.

"Of course it was. Thank you."

Reaching up on my tiptoes, he leans down to meet my lips. The kiss is short and sweet because anything more than that, and I'd let him fuck me inside the shower.

What's so bad about that? I have no other plans tonight.

I shake my head. This is ridiculous. We can't have sex every waking moment. I mean, we *can* but I have to draw the line somewhere. The bond clearly has other plans.

"Okay. Go away now. I need to wash between my legs. I feel... sticky. I'm pretty sure your cum is still coating my thighs."

He smirks proudly at that.

"I could wash you," Thorne offers.

"Rain check?"

I let go of Thorne and return to the shower's spray. A loud smack fills the air, and a searing pain spreads over my ass cheeks.

That mother fucker spanked me!

Chapter 12 - Vara

It's been three months since Layla, Thorne, and I first fucked. Three months since our discussion about fated mates.

We've been busy nearly every night, only getting one night a week, if that, to spend time together. Most of the time, we'd fool around in the SUV while heading to and from meetings or events. Or sometimes, Layla let us lay her down on the conference room table after a SUC meeting to feast on her delectable cunt.

Tonight it's just Layla and me.

We're in an SUV heading home from a human networking event. Thorne wasn't able to escort us this time, being called away by Xander for some gargoyle business, whatever that means, so he left his right-hand man in charge.

The griffin whose name I can't remember sits up front, scowling. I ignore him, since griffins are the grumpiest of supes and rarely speak. It's why they like to take on security roles where all they have to do is stand in the background, silent and invisible.

Layla's hand is in mine, and she sighs.

"What is it, Bug?"

She scrunches her nose at the nickname, which sends my heart fluttering. She's a beautiful woman, strong and powerful, but she's also an adorable bug.

And a bunny, as Thorne likes to call her.

"Do you ever wonder how we all would have met if the elders hadn't come up with this unveiling plan?"

I bring her hand up to my mouth and kiss her knuckles. Her fangs peek out through the smile she gives me.

All her smiles are wonderful gifts.

"Destiny would have found a way. I'm sure you and Thorne would have eventually met through King Basque since you're the new vampire queen."

"I was Millie's royal advisor for decades and met with Xander and Locheran many times before now. The king never brought Thorne around."

She lays her head on my shoulder, and I close my eyes. It's such a small thing, having her find comfort in my touch and my nearness. But I relish it.

"We can't dwell on the what ifs. We're all here together now."

As for me, if there had been no unification plan, I might have become desperate enough to sneak my way back into Layla's life and vie for a spot on her protection team. Sphinxes are guardians first and foremost.

Except, that's not who I am anymore. I'm successful, powerful. I have my own protection team when I'm out in public. I haven't been a guardian in a very long time. I always felt inadequate in the role, never passionate enough. That's not the case with Layla. I would end lives without a second thought if it meant she is safe to show me that bright smile of hers again.

When we arrive at her penthouse, we silently ascend in the elevator. She's exhausted. I am too. We've been working hard on this unveiling plan, putting all our social spoons in one basket as we attend these events where we're required to slap on smiles and exude happiness and politeness.

Layla's better at it than I am. She's the sunshine to my darkness. Long ago, humans believed sphinx to be sun deities. I enjoy the sun just fine... but I've always been drawn to the moon. Now I wonder if that has something to do with Layla and Thorne who are both bound to the night.

After Layla's guards do a security sweep, they let us in. She immediately kicks them out, even the young vampire who has a room in the penthouse.

"Come back shortly before sunrise," she tells him, closing the door in his face.

"And what do you have planned that will take until sunrise?" I ask once we walk into the kitchen.

A sinister smile spreads across my face because I know exactly what she has planned.

"It's come to my attention that this is the first time we've had time to ourselves—just you and me."

Layla extracts two wine glasses from the cabinets and fills them.

"That's true."

"And I want to do something... a little different tonight."

Her fangs are out, and she teases her plump bottom lip with the pointed tip.

"Oh?"

She shifts on her feet, unsure of how to ask for what she wants. I don't need to ask her what she wants—*I know*.

"You're usually in control..." Her words trail off, and she twirls a piece of hair at the nape of her neck.

I clutch her chin.

"Use your words, darling. Tell me what you want."

She closes her eyes and when they open, they're pitch black.

"Can I be in control tonight?"

I ghost my lips over hers, and she whimpers.

"You never have to ask, Layla. I will gladly take orders from you."

To show her just how true those words are, I get on my knees before her and place my palms on my thighs.

I keep my eyes straight ahead, waiting for instructions.

"Holy hell, V... that's fucking hot."

I stifle the urge to roll my eyes. She wants to be in control, but she's being silly. I'd spank her if I was the one calling the shots tonight.

Layla said she likes to be in control in the bedroom, but it's clear she's submissive. She always defers to me when we're together with Thorne. I think she puts on an act and pretends to enjoy dominating a lover. She likely takes control to protect herself and it's because of her past with her husband and her sire.

She's yet to tell us more about that time in her life.

Layla's strong vampire hand wraps around my throat and squeezes. My mouth opens and Layla spits in it, sending a shot of lust throughout my body.

My eyes widen, not expecting that.

But, fuck, it was sexy.

"Take off my clothes, then bury your face in my pussy," she says and kisses me.

When she releases my lips and throat, I stand, and she turns so I can unzip her out of her dress. It's a body-hugging gown that has had me drooling from the moment she walked into the living room after getting dressed.

And, of course, she's wearing nothing underneath.

"I knew you weren't wearing underwear. I could smell how wet you were for me all night long."

She smirks, then points to her bedroom. I lead the way, and she follows. Once there, I turn to wait for orders.

"On your knees."

I begin to remove my clothes, but Layla snatches the tail of my braid and tugs my head back.

"Did I say you could undress?"

Oh... okay. Maybe I was wrong about Layla being submissive. She's a switch for sure. I think being with me and Thorne has awakened her full dominant potential.

"Apologies, my queen," I say and lower to my knees.

She gets on the bed and opens her legs.

"Now... make me come."

I descend on her like the monster I am, burying my nose into her sweet sex and inhaling deeply.

A growl that I haven't unleashed in centuries bursts from my lips. I use my fingers to spread her pussy lips open and delve my tongue inside, lapping up her sweet taste.

She moans and arches her back, clutching my braid and tugging me closer.

While I feast, my tail swoops in and plays with one of her nipples. She gasps when my fingertip finds her clit, massaging the sensitive bundle of nerves in circles.

"Oh, God, Vara," she screams.

My wings expand as Layla's pleasure rolls through me, my feathers shuddering with every thrust of my tongue. My arms are wrapped around her thick thighs, and my claws dig in hard enough to break skin. Blood trails down, dripping onto the black rug underneath my knees.

After Layla shakes with her first orgasm, I come up for air.

I need another one from her.

I shove a finger inside her precious pussy and start pumping in and out, but this time, I don't retract my claws.

A string of unintelligible words spews out of Layla's mouth, her eyes rolling back into her head.

"You like that, Bug? You like a little pain with your pleasure?"

"Y-yesss... y-yeah... p-please."

Blood coats my fingers and paw as I continue to fuck her, slicing her walls with my claws with every pass.

The cuts will heal within minutes.

I cover her clit with my mouth and lash it with my tongue.

"I'm going to come again," she groans.

I pick up speed, my sharp fingers pumping in and out of her brutally. When I hum against her clit, she's sent over the edge.

I remove my fingers and lick them clean of her blood and juices, then lap up her bloody slit.

Layla lifts me off the floor and crashes her lips against mine. I open for her, allowing her tongue to caress my own. She moans, tasting her blood and cum on my lips.

We kiss until our lips are puffy. When she pulls away, she points at the bed.

"Undress and get in the center."

I nod curtly. "Yes, my queen."

Layla's eyes are still pitch black; her fangs bared as she watches me slip out of the red negligee I call a dress. My hard nipples ache, begging for attention.

I get into my spot on the center of the bed and open my legs. Layla smirks and crawls in between them. She leans over to wrap her hand around my throat and squeezes hard as she places a gentle kiss on my lips.

"You are so beautiful, Vara."

Releasing her hold, she brushes her lips across my chin and down my neck until reaching a breast. She takes a nipple into her mouth and laps her tongue over the hardened tip.

"You are so mine," she says, echoing the words Thorne and I have said to her.

She presses two fingers inside me, and my eyes roll into the back of my head as she pumps in and out slowly. Her mouth continues to work my nipple, her fangs scratching over my furred skin enough to draw blood. She licks the welled drops immediately and groans.

"You taste fucking amazing," she says, adding a third finger and picking up speed.

My tail moves behind Layla and presses against her wet opening. I don't wait for orders and harden the tip to slip it inside her.

"Fuck," she murmurs, against my breast.

We fall into a frantic rhythm, her fingers filling me and my tail pounding into her. She shakes with her orgasm first, and I remove my tail to suck her sweet juices off the tip. Her pleasure rolls through me like a wave of ecstasy... a high I've never reached with any drug in existence.

"Come for me, Vara," Layla says, adding yet another finger.

She's unrelenting with her thrusts.

"Fuck, Lollipop. That's good."

I vaguely hear the door to the penthouse open and Thorne calls out. The thought of him watching us, but not touching—not participating, nearly sends me over the edge.

"Thorne," I gasp.

"I know," Layla says, but doesn't let up.

The air in the room seems to electrify the moment the gargoyle finds us.

"Watch."

It's all Layla says as she readjusts herself to cover my clit with her mouth. She's not being gentle with her plump lips or her greedy fingers. My pussy pulses with need.

"I'm close, darling," I groan.

Glancing over Layla's shoulder, I spot Thorne leaned up against the wall, watching like a good boy.

Layla's tongue thrashes perfectly against my clit and when she reaches her free hand up to pinch and pull my nipple; I erupt with my orgasm. My entire body quakes, stars crossing my vision, and I squirt all over Layla's hand.

I don't think I've ever squirted before. At least, not like *this.*

Layla stares up at me, smirking and proud of herself.

"Such a good girl, V, coming so hard for me."

She crawls off the bed and walks over to Thorne, sliding her fingers coated with my cum into his mouth. He closes his eyes, whimpering as he sucks. Once he's done, Layla returns to the bed and holds out her hand. I take it, and she pulls me up.

"Now Thorne is going to clean us in the shower, then he'll change the sheets so we can all cuddle and talk after."

She doesn't give him the option to protest, not that he would, and leads us all into the bathroom.

Chapter 13 - Layla

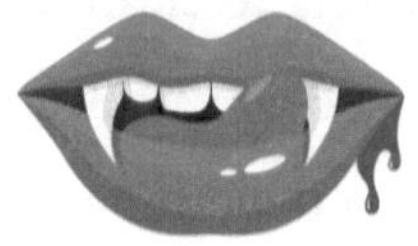

That was empowering. Vara letting me take control reminded me just how far I've come, not only in accepting my sexuality, but my body and my desires.

Thorne washed both of us clean and when I tried to reward him with a blow job, he refused, saying tonight was about us, not him. Then we dressed in sleep clothes and now all three of us are cuddled in my king-sized bed with Thorne in between me and Vara.

He's the biggest so it's easier for both of us to curl up against his sides.

"Tell us why you were hesitant to ask for what you wanted earlier?" Vara says after we settle underneath the covers.

I knew she was going to ask me this.

I've yet to open up to the both of them. To be fair, Vara and Thorne haven't shared much of their lives either. Vara is stubborn, and Thorne is a man of few words.

I won't push them. They'll share when they're ready.

"I told you my husband was a nightmare, right?" Thorne tenses underneath me while Vara hums a yes. "He was abusive, physically and verbally. He'd demean me every chance he got. I let his words tear me down and it took a long time to build myself back up. When I finally convinced myself that I was good enough and deserved to be happy, I got sick."

I hate thinking about my past. I've worked through the worst of it, but I guess it's hard to let it all go. My hesitation to ask for what I wanted is clear of that.

"I thought being turned would mean I was finally free. Diago, my sire, had other plans. For two weeks after he turned me, I lived through hell. He was just as cruel and controlling as my husband, only worse because he was inhuman... he was stronger and had no morals.

"I can't fathom reliving the details, maybe I'll share it with you both one day. What I can say is that Diago did everything he could to break me, but I wasn't going to let another man shatter my will. Not after I worked so hard to love myself. I lashed out at him. He'd expected me to be weak and compliant—sires are able to control their fledglings—but, for some reason, I never fell under his compulsion.

"I always wondered why Diago couldn't control me. Maybe it was because I was destined for greater things. Or maybe me being sick with the plague prevented that part of the turning from taking hold. Whatever the reason, I was grateful. So, I pretended to be controlled by him, and when his caution fell, I broke a wooden chair and drove a piece of it into his heart."

Thorne kisses my temple, and Vara reaches her arm across his stomach so she can palm my arm that I have resting against Thorne's side.

"He was supposed to be my guide into this immortal life, teaching me to control my thirst. I had no one. I learned to manage my hunger on my own; I don't know how I did it. I even managed not to kill innocent lives in the process.

"But I was so fucking angry—at my abusive husband and my cruel sire. Every vampire I met along the way saw my fury as a weapon and utilized it. I became a warrior, mostly against hunters who aimed to kill our kind or other supes who posed a threat.

"I moved to the U.S. in 1921 after hearing about vampires settling in New Orleans. I found a job and went through the motions of living. Then a year later, Millie and I met. She was in New Orleans for a WOVE event and showed up with other important vampires at the jazz club where I sang. The moment I finished my performance, Millie pulled me aside. She immediately saw how lost I was. How the anger was wearing me down. We became fast lovers, but as vampires, it was merely physical. We care for each other, and are loyal to one another, but the deep emotions of love were never there. Neither of us wanted to be without the other so I followed Millie back to New York City and became her royal advisor.

"I think she's the reason why I'm no longer angry. Now I smile and laugh, and I *enjoy* life."

I shift and lift up on my elbow so I can see my two mates.

"Control comes easily if it's just sex, no emotions, but with you two... Vara you're different than any lover I've had. When you take control, it's not for your pleasure... it's for *mine. Ours.* I wasn't sure if I could be as good as you—"

"It was good. So very good," Vara says, leaning over Thorne to clutch my chin. "Don't ever doubt that... do you understand me, Layla Sophia Aldana?"

Her words cause an ache in my chest. I swear my heart flutters.

"I understand."

She stares into my eyes as if looking for the truth embedded within my soul. When she believes me, she gives me a quick nod.

"Good," she sighs and lays her head back on Thorne's shoulder. "Now, let's enjoy this rare time together. We have a busy couple of months left until we can explore the bond."

The bond.

Every day it calls to us. I know they feel it too... the near painful pull... the overactive sex drive (it's ridiculous how horny I am. All. The. Time.)

Thorne is the first to fall asleep then Vara. I watch them at peace until my eyes start to droop. It's crazy to think that these two beautiful beings are mine. They want *me*. I lived my entire life feeling as if nowhere was home. I think it's because I was missing two important parts.

My two guardians.

The ones who protect my body... my heart... my soul.

Chapter 14 - Thorne

I'm smiling.

I can't remember the last time I've smiled this much.

It's been five and a half months since I assumed the role as Layla's head of security. Five and a half months since meeting these two beautiful creatures.

Unfortunately, we haven't been able to spend much time together. Despite Vara taking a step back from her clubs, she still has responsibilities with her new role on the committee. She's out nearly every night making connections. Layla has been busy attending functions as well, and that's on top of tending to her royal vampire duties.

As Layla's head of security, and now mate, I've had to limit my time around her again. All I want to do when in her presence is give her multiple orgasms, which takes away from my role to protect her, so I've assigned my next best guard to escort her to the majority of her public events.

Any chance the three of us has had to fuck has been quick, mostly happening in the back of a car or on the table after a SUC meeting. We've been careful not to come simultaneously since the one time that happened, we all passed out.

Tonight is the first night in a month that none of us have obligations. We're at Layla's penthouse where I'm cooking dinner for Vara and myself, and Layla is sitting at the kitchen island sipping on wine.

"I love your smile," Layla says dreamily. "You've been doing it more."

"It's true. You have," Vara says, glancing up from her laptop. She's always working, even when she's off, but she never misses a word we say. "Unfortunately, I find it rather endearing."

"You just hate to admit you like us," Layla teases.

Vara shrugs. "Sphinxes are very loving creatures. I just didn't have anyone to offer my love and care to until now."

"Love?" Layla asks, her voice slightly higher with a hint of panic.

"Please, don't be so human about this, Lollipop. We're mates. Of course we'll fall in love."

I must have made a face or some sort of noise because Vara turns to me.

"You have doubts too, Thorne?"

While it's true Layla and Vara are awakening something inside me, love is something I never imagined I'd experience. Not since my entire family was killed by hunters.

It's been almost a hundred years.

It feels like it's been a thousand.

When I don't answer, Vara continues with caution. "I see the haunted look on your face anytime you look at us. You hide it well from others, but I recognize that mask you wear because I wear the same one. You're scared to love us because you're worried you'll lose us. We've *all* lived long lives full of loss. It's understandable to be hesitant to accept this."

She's absolutely right. I've suffered too many losses... too many heartbreaks in my life.

Gargoyles are born to protect. We know that many of our kind fall to an early grave, mostly through battles against evil, but that doesn't make it easier to mourn the losses.

I fought alongside my brothers. I protected cities my father and mother once protected. They all suffered many life-threatening injuries, but it wasn't a battle that ended their lives. We might be immortal and can live for centuries, but we can still die. For me, it's by decapitation or a warspear to the heart.

"Voice your thoughts, Thorne. We're here to listen," Layla says, placing her palm on my forearm. I'm cutting up vegetables for the stir fry dish I'm making, and pause, sighing with my entire body at Layla's touch.

"I was just thinking about the time I nearly died."

"Is that how you got the scar?" Vara asks, closing her laptop and folding her arms over her chest.

"It is. It happened during a battle against a demon trying to kidnap humans to enslave them. He sliced me on the face with a warspear. The weapons are made with iron which is toxic to gargoyles. I was poisoned and ill for months. But I lived."

I glance up at Vara, her brows pinched while listening to my story.

"My family, however, was not so lucky. I lost them in 1922."

"I'm so sorry, Thorne," Layla says, sorrow claiming her voice.

"Rumors of our existence began spreading amongst the humans in Europe. Hunters formed to seek us out. They tracked down and killed all supernatural beings, but some of these humans focused on gargoyles after believing our horns would bring good luck and ward off evil spirits. It's clear the legends of our species have been misinterpreted poorly. Our horns do no such thing."

I stop speaking as an ache forms in my throat. Tears threaten to fall despite it being decades since I've mourned my family.

I pick up a pile of cut vegetables and turn to the pan heating on the stove to toss them in.

"My parents were taken one night while on patrol. The hunters... they knew how to incapacitate gargoyles and used an iron wrought net to trap them. I was the youngest amongst my siblings, so I was ordered to stay and protect the small village in France that my family had been assigned to watch over. My brothers left to save them." I swallow hard. "None of them returned. They were all murdered. I found their bodies. Their horns were taken."

Layla wraps her arms around my waist, resting her head between my tucked wings. I relish her touch. It's cold yet warms me throughout. Vara stands off to the side, her tail caressing my arm. I smile because it's such a Vara thing to do. She's keeping her distance while letting me know she's here for me.

Clearing my throat, I continue. "The Council of Gargoyle Elders ordered me to leave the village immediately for my safety. They said there had been similar incidents of gargoyles being killed by hunters. That prompted the Council to change the rules."

I let the veggies simmer and peel Layla off my back, making sure to give her a quick kiss before she sits down at the kitchen island.

"Entire families could no longer protect villages or cities together. There are exceptions. If the city is large like Paris or New York, then up to three relatives can be in the same army. Only towns with populations of at least ten thousand will be guarded and there must be at least two gargoyle guards on patrol so one is never left vulnerable. And we must stay masked around humans at all times."

I check on the egg rolls baking in the oven. Satisfied they're done, I turn off the heat and keep them in there to stay warm while waiting for the stir fry to finish.

"When I joined Xander's army shortly after my family was slaughtered, I hadn't expected anything more than the camaraderie of my fellow fighters. I wasn't looking for replacements. Though Locheran treats me like a brother, and he's annoyingly loud and hyper like one of my older brothers had been."

I frown at the thought.

Locheran and Xander are the closest I have to brothers now. Locheran drags me out to human bars and clubs, sometimes Xander even goes. Or, at least, he did before meeting his mate. We've had plenty of poker nights or nights where we talk about the battles we've fought and compared our goriest kills.

Everything's changing, though, with me in this new role and Xander focusing on his mate.

And me focusing on *my* mates.

"So, I don't trust easily, and I don't offer my love often. That being said, what I feel for the both of you is nothing like I've experienced before."

"Have you ever been in love? Not the love of family or friends but *romantic* love?" Vara asks, grabbing a beer from the fridge.

She opens it with ease and hands it to me. She knows I don't drink often, but tonight I need it. Even if it's just one or two to relax me.

I shrug. "I suppose not. Is love supposed to hurt? Because that's how this feels, especially when you two aren't here. I know it's the bond, tethering us. But I also feel protective and jealous. I can't even count how many times I've had to stop myself from tearing someone to shreds anytime they got too close to either of you."

"I know what you mean," Layla laughs. "Teddy and Millie have a crush on you, Thorne, and I want to rip their eyes from their heads anytime they check you out."

I stand taller.

"They think I'm cute?"

She shakes her head. "The words they used were hot. Godly."

"I've met Gods," Vara scoffs. "They're beautiful but assholes. Thorne is beautiful and kind."

"I think you mean dangerous and sexy," I say, puffing out my chest.

"Please," Vara chuckles. "Don't be toxic. Besides, I have no doubt you could rip a spine from a body. But you're also delicate and considerate, especially when it comes to pleasuring us."

Vara waves her hand toward the stove.

"And you can cook."

"A lot of immortals can cook," I say, amused. "We have time to learn to be great at a lot of things."

"Then please share with the class the other talents you have." Layla's face lights up at the prospect.

My cheeks warm because it's been far too long since I've shared such personal details about myself. I've already talked more tonight than I typically speak in an entire week.

But with Layla and Vara, it comes naturally.

"I like to sing, and I think I'm decent at it. I can also play several instruments: piano, guitar, drums."

Layla gasps. "Well now you have to sing for us. I have a piano in the sitting room."

My phone dings with a text from a guard letting me know someone is here at the entrance of the penthouse.

Layla's dinner.

"After we eat," I say, giving the vampire a wink.

I leave to retrieve the human. This donor is a tall and slender man with pale skin, which means he donates often. When I bring him to the kitchen island, Layla's eyes darken, and her fangs drop.

"Thorne," she whispers. "You got me dinner?"

"Of course, Bunny," I say, palming her cheek.

I point at the stool next to Layla and the human sits. I return to the food on the stove. The stir fry is done so I scoop it out of the pan into two waiting bowls, then retrieve the egg rolls from the oven, dropping two on each pile of food.

I bring the dishes to the island where we all like to eat, instead of at the dining room table, which feels far too formal. After refilling Vara's wine glass, I grab my beer and sit down.

I relish the sweet sounds Vara makes as she tastes the food I cooked. Typically, my meals are quick, an afterthought. Or I order takeout from a restaurant. I can't even remember the last time I prepared dinner for someone I cared about.

Despite Layla not being able to consume human food, I didn't want her to feel left out, so I contacted her assistant, and she ordered the donor.

Layla takes the human's arm and drinks from his wrist. She sighs as she locks eyes with me.

Desire and appreciation look back at me.

Contentment.

This must be what love is. It's a strange feeling. Different from loving my friends and family. I would die for friends and family, but for my mates, I would lay waste to the world.

Chapter 15 - Vara

Over 2,000 years of living on this godforsaken Earth; I've experienced loss, lust, and vengeance.

Never have I loved.

Not the kind that consumes the body until all thoughts and desires belong to the beings that claim your soul.

My soul.

It belongs to them.

Thorne and Layla are my mates. It's clearer every day.

Like right now.

I'd never willingly cuddle up in a chair with a vampire on my lap while a gargoyle serenades us.

Thorne's fingers expertly dance across the piano's keys as he belts out *When a Man Loves a Woman* by Percy Sledge. He also changed the lyrics to say *two* women and switched all instances of 'she' to either they or them.

I roll my eyes at how adorable that is.

The gargoyle amuses me. He's broody as fuck when he's around anyone other than Layla and me. We get to see this special side of him. His smile that's a little lopsided. His dark blue eyes that always look haunted brighten when he's with us.

I hadn't expected to be so attracted to him. I honestly thought Layla was the center of our bond, and my appeal for Thorne was only because of her. But I find my feelings for him to be equally as strong as the ones I have for Layla.

Do they both feel the same?

Layla's face is lit up with the biggest smile I've ever seen. Her hands are clasped in front of her as she watches Thorne play the piano and sing. She glances up at me every once in a while, as if making sure I'm also enjoying the one man show.

When Thorne ends the song, she claps enthusiastically, bouncing in her seat on top of me. I ignore the spark of desire that rolls through me... until remembering that my mates and I share pleasure.

They turn their heads to me, eyes darkening and fangs bared.

"V," Layla purrs. She leans in and brushes her lips over my neck. "Do you need us right now?"

"I always need you," I say, gasping as Layla's cold hands slide down my chest and stomach before cupping my pussy.

She pushes past the thin layer of cloth that barely qualifies as underwear and slips her finger inside me. The chill of her skin in my heat makes me shudder.

"So wet for us," Layla hums, pumping in and out slowly. "Here's what's going to happen."

My cunt clamps down around her fingers at her demanding tone. I just love when she's a boss.

"Thorne and I are going to make you come. Then we're all going to cuddle and talk some more, because you've been holding out on us."

Her thumb grazes my clit, and I arch off the chair.

"I want to know about all your adventures." She kisses my neck. "All your hardships." A kiss to my sternum. "And all your desires."

Layla covers the peak of my breast with her mouth and bites down. I scream as pain ripples from the wound, but it quickly turns into pleasure as she drinks from me while lashing her tongue over my taut nipple.

Her fingers pump into me faster, harder, and I close my eyes.

When Layla has had enough of my blood, she unlatches from my tit and removes her fingers. Seconds later, I'm being lifted off the chair. Thorne sits back down with me on his lap. He spreads my legs open wide, and Layla settles between them.

The tip of Thorne's tail finds my asshole. It's self-lubricating, and he slathers it up and down to prepare me.

Oh fuck.

I might like to be in control, but submitting to my mates is... nice. I let myself relax into Thorne's hard body. My wings have unwillingly extended, too weak with pleasure to keep them against my back. They don't get in the way as Thorne undresses me, ripping off my sheer top to cover my breasts with his hands.

Layla's bite wound hasn't healed completely and while it's no longer bleeding, it still aches as Thorne pinches and pulls my nipples.

A pleasurable pain.

I look down my body, watching as Layla slides two fingers inside me. With her other hand, she fishes Thorne's bulbous cock from his sweats and fists it. Then she guides the tip to my asshole. I scream out when Thorne slides into me, in one quick thrust, to the hilt. He fucks me slowly at first, then finds a rhythm in tandem with Layla's fingers. Neither of them is holding back.

"Holy shit. Fuck."

"That's it, V," Layla says. "Let us hear how well we fuck you."

Her mouth descends on my clit, sucking it into her mouth and lashing her tongue over the sensitive bundle of nerves.

"You're so fucking good at that, Lollipop."

She whimpers at my praise and adds a third finger, moaning as our shared pleasure intensifies. I groan at the vibration of Layla's moan against my clit and bury my hands into her hair, gripping the curly strands roughly as Thorne pounds into my ass. The gargoyle's hands are still playing with my breasts, pinching and pulling my aching nipples. His tail whips around behind Layla, anxious to be part of the action.

"Put it inside her, Thorne," I say between gasps.

Layla's still wearing shorts, and I smile when I hear the fabric rip. She jerks and moans when Thorne's tail slides into her.

We're a tangled mess of sex.

A gargoyle cock in my ass, his tail in our mate's pussy, the vampire's fingers inside my cunt, and her mouth on my clit.

The moment Thorne picks up speed, deliciously destroying my asshole with his thrusts, I reach my orgasm. My walls clamp down on Layla's fingers and once I'm done shaking, she removes them and shoves them into Thorne's mouth so he can lick them clean.

That's when he comes, his cock jerking as cum splatters the inside of my asshole. Stars burst over my vision for a second time, blackness threatening to take over.

Thankfully, I don't pass out.

I watch, drunk off the ecstasy of two orgasms, as Layla chases her release. Her eyes are black, mouth open, and fangs out. Thorne's tail starts vibrating, fucking her rigorously. I tug down the material of her tank top and pinch her nipple, sending her over the edge.

Layla collapses on top of me, a silly grin on her face. Thorne tucks his cock back into his pants before adjusting us so we're both laying on top of his wide and muscular body.

My wings have retreated to my back, but Thorne's wings are now out. He cocoons us inside while we bask in the headiness of our orgasms.

My heart beats a little faster. Layla puts her palm over my chest while Thorne caresses our arms with his palms.

We all sigh at the same time.

Fuck.

I'm in love with these two.

I don't remember falling asleep, but I wake still wrapped in Thorne's wings and arms. Layla is beside me, staring at me with a smile.

"You look peaceful when you sleep," she says.

My eyes widen, causing her smile to falter.

"What is it?"

Thorne must have been listening to our conversation, hearing Layla's concern, because he releases us from his hold. I sit up and rub my hands over my face.

"How long was I out?"

Layla glances at her phone. "About three hours."

"What is it, Vara? You can tell us." Thorne says, his deep voice calming the panic swirling inside my chest.

I sigh. "Sleep doesn't come easily for me. I toss and turn while trying to shut off my brain and by the time I finally fall asleep, I'm awakened by a nightmare. I typically only get a few hours of sleep per night."

I stand and walk into the kitchen for a glass of water. Thorne and Layla follow.

"Your hands are shaking," Layla whispers, watching me gulp down the water.

When I set the empty glass on the marble countertop, she takes my hand. Thorne is beside her, his eyebrows pinched.

"It's the first time in hundreds of years since I've slept so peacefully. No dreams, no nightmares. I'm rested and happy, but I'm also freaking out just a little bit."

Layla laughs. She *laughs.*

"Sorry," she says, covering her mouth with her free hand, which Thorne immediately pulls down. "I've never seen you..."

She waves a hand up and down my body.

"Panicked. Vulnerable."

I scoff.

She buries her face into both of her hands this time, shaking her head.

"Ugh, I'm not explaining myself well. I just mean that it's okay to be vulnerable and weak sometimes. You don't always have to be defiant and strong, Vara." She steps to me and reaches up to cradle my face. "Tell us why you're freaking out about this. Because I bet it has something to do with you always relying on yourself and never having anyone to watch over you."

Shit.

She's right.

Thorne grabs my empty glass and refills it, and I take a sip of the water when he hands it back to me.

"I'm old; 2,056 years on this Earth. The first couple hundred years were wonderful. I had a family: parents, siblings. I was to wed the son of a prominent sphinx couple and have a litter of kits. I was happy for the most part. My family were guardians for temples in the southern region of Egypt. We took pride in that job. Until humans discovered us. They found one of our golden feathers. My parents were killed first, then my sisters. I was the youngest, the fastest, so I fled. Like a fucking coward, I let them die. I didn't save them."

My eyes find Thorne's, and I realize our stories are eerily similar. Both of our lives have been ruined by human hunters, our families murdered because of their greed. I think that's why I'm so passionate about this unveiling plan. It will offer protections for us. At least, that's the hope.

"I hid away in a cave for hundreds of years and when I emerged, my species had been slaughtered. The sphinx I was set to marry, gone. The temples I was destined to protect, looted and destroyed. I had failed on so many levels. A lot of innocent humans also died, all because of the greedy men who murdered everyone I knew and loved for golden feathers."

Layla's arm wraps around my waist, and she leans her head on my chest. Thorne is on my other side and since he's slightly taller than me, I'm able to lean into him.

Their nearness, their touch, soothes me until I'm no longer shaking.

"I tried to move on. I had to. But I was broken. I had nothing. All my belongings were stolen by the hunters. I was forced to pluck my own golden feathers to melt down and sell for money. Do you know how painful that is for a sphinx? It took years to amass a small fortune. I surrounded myself with luxury and supernatural beings, but I never let any of them get close. I knew that one day, hunters would find me again. I was careful to mask myself when around humans, but it only took one time showing my true form to a human I thought I could trust. They betrayed me. They told others about my golden feathers and once again I was hunted. I fled to America. I heard about a fast-growing metropolis led by a vampire queen named Mildred. How easy it was to hide amid tall buildings and within crowded sidewalks. I arrived in New York City and pleaded with her to give me sanctuary.

"It was actually her idea that I should open nightclubs for supernatural beings. Places we could go with no judgment, where we could be safe. I found witches to set up wards and laid out some ground rules, and nearly a dozen clubs later, here I am."

Layla frowns. "And your sleep?"

"Centuries of loss, you're bound to be haunted by those you once loved. They live in my dreams but most of the time, I relive seeing them slaughtered. I was there when it happened. I was crouched in a tree as knives were plunged into my parents' chests. As my sisters' heads were both chopped off. Sometimes their deaths play on repeat, in both my waking and sleeping hours."

A bell rings, notifying us that the sun will soon be rising. Layla's UV protection shades begin lowering.

"Right, well, I didn't mean for a wonderful night together to end so... morbidly."

"We all have similar horrors that we lived through, but at least we have each other now," Layla says, smiling and squeezing my hand. "We will never have to go through life alone again. You do realize that, Vara, don't you?"

I nod. "It's still strange, and it might take me a while to get used to it, but waking up after a few hours of peaceful sleep with you by my side, both of us in Thorne's arms, was more than I could have ever asked for."

My phone rings, and I scowl.

"I know you two are about to retire for the day. I wish I could stay. I have a few daytime human networking events to attend. I know you have some meetings tonight and a week full of events."

Layla pouts, and I clutch her chin, running my clawed thumb over her bottom lip.

"Don't worry, Bug, I'll see you Friday at the unity event."

It'll be the first big event with high-profile humans who we've formed relationships with. Friday will be the test. We'll reveal ourselves to them, introduce them to other supernatural beings and gauge their reaction. We're not worried about them exposing us to the world. These humans have reputations to uphold. They're not going to risk sounding insane by telling people of our existence, no matter how true it is.

I just want to get this over with so I can live the rest of my life with my mates. The question, though, will that be in a peaceful world, or one ravaged with war?

Chapter 16 - Layla

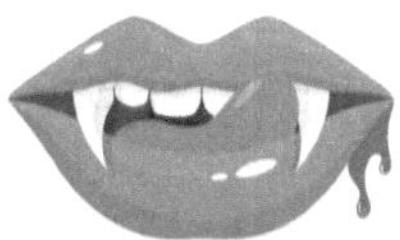

The week went by quickly thanks to a busy schedule of meetings and events.

Thorne is still keeping his distance, sending his best guard in place to protect me when I'm out in public. He claims it's necessary since he can barely control himself when around me.

The longer we go without completing the bond, the harder it will get to stay away from each other.

We desperately want to find someone who knows about a three-way bond, just so we can be as informed as possible. But if Vara is over 2,000 years old and has never heard of one herself, then it's merely hopeless.

We'll have to experiment, and we can't do that for another week or so when meetings and events for the Supernatural Unveiling Plan are more spread out. Especially since we don't know how long we'll be out of commission while giving ourselves to each other to satisfy and intensify the bond.

I walk out of my bedroom after changing into my gown for tonight's event. It's dark green with a tulle skirt and beaded embroidery along the long-sleeved top. My hair is styled to the side, my reddish-brown curls falling over my shoulder.

In the living room, I find Thorne with his arms crossed while staring out of one of my floor-to-ceiling windows.

"You're being extra broody, Thorne," I say and giggle.

When he turns, I fluff out my skirt and do a little spin.

"How do I look?"

His eyes widen, his breathing becoming heavy as he scans me head to toe.

"I'm guessing by your growl that you like."

"I very much like."

"Well, I very much like *you* in this suit," I say, checking him out from head to toe.

The suit is all black and sexy as hell against his purple skin. His hair is up in an elegant man bun, and his wings are out instead of having them tucked against his back like usual.

"Everything okay?"

"Yes, why?"

I move to run my hand down his wing, but he grabs my wrist, stopping me.

"We'll be late if you touch them."

"What will happen?" I bite my lip. "Would it turn you on?"

He puts the wings away, and I frown.

"Not only will it turn me on, but your touch will make me feral. I'll rip this dress off you and fuck you up against the window. Or I'll fold you over the couch and take you from behind. Gargoyle wings are highly sensitive to their mate's touch."

I realize he hasn't let Vara or me touch them during sex yet. I know how important they are to him. But Thorne never puts himself first when it comes to pleasure.

That's going to change tonight.

"Well," I say, lust attempting to capture my voice. "I guess Vara and I will need to pay them extra attention the next time we're together."

I give him a wink and grab my purse from the table before heading to the door.

We walk into a small ballroom at Lanthom Hotel in Midtown. A decent crowd has already formed, enough that Thorne stays by my side, holding my hand as we weave through bodies. The rest of my team huddles around me. I tried to convince Thorne that I no longer needed such an extravagant security team, but he disagreed and added a few more members to tonight's detail.

The brat.

I spot King Basque near the middle of the room, speaking with a few other supes: a fae, a witch, and a wolf shifter. Not many supernaturals were invited tonight, only SUC members and a handful of other supe leaders. We're still not ready to extend this plan to the entire community.

Xander's mate is also here, clutching his arm as if her life depends on it. I somehow missed meeting her at the party I hosted months ago.

I suppose I *was* a little distracted while getting tail fucked on the dance floor.

As I approach, the supes chatting with the couple wrap up their conversation and disperse.

"Xander," I say once I reach him. He's already told me to call him by his first name anytime we're at these events. He claims King Basque is his father.

My eyes immediately fall to the short, plus-size woman in the stunning purple cocktail dress. It has sheer sleeves that fall off her shoulders and showcase her lovely tattoos: heather flowers and Evangeline lilacs.

She's gorgeous.

"I agree," Xander says with a chuckle.

"I did *not* mean to say that out loud, even though it's absolutely true." I stifle the urge to cover my mouth and hide my smile, but Thorne is still holding my hand, and he squeezes it as if anticipating the move.

Xander notices our embrace but doesn't say a word about it. Thorne also doesn't make a move to release me despite noticing Xander's rapt stare.

"I'm Evangeline," the human says, extending her hand to me.

I take it, and she hisses.

"Cold," she says under her breath.

"Unfortunately, it's a side effect of being dead." I laugh, noticing the lovely blush that spreads across her cheeks. "You're not quite human, are you?"

There was a zap of magic between us when I accepted her greeting.

"Well, mating with Xander gave me immortality and his healing abilities. But my mother is also a witch, so she thinks I have some power within me that's trying to wake up." She holds up her palm and in the middle is a marking that looks like a daisy. "She gave me this, and I can basically shoot light lasers out of it."

Xander clears his throat and pushes Evangeline's arm down out of sight.

"Kitten, please. Supernatural hearing in this room. I don't want everyone knowing about my secret little weapon."

Kitten. That's a cute nickname. She blushes again, and I realize I like this woman. Millie and I should invite her to a get-together sometime. Maybe we can have a dinner party with our mates.

"So..." Xander says, glancing down at Thorne still holding my hand. "What we talked about is true?"

"Yes," Thorne says without hesitation.

Thorne mentioned that he asked Xander if he'd ever heard of a three-way mate situation. Just like Vara, he hadn't.

Evangeline scours the room. "I was hoping to meet Vara."

"What about me?" Vara says, seemingly manifesting behind Evangeline. The short woman jumps and yelps and Xander's quick to throw a punch. Vara catches it with ease. "Sorry, Your Majesty. Didn't mean to startle the little one. Good reflexes though."

Evangeline's eyes widen as Vara walks around to stand next to Thorne, placing her hand on his shoulder.

"Wait, I thought you were a sphinx," Evangeline states.

"I'm masked, darling," Vara says, giving her a smile. Once again, the human blushes. She's adorable. "Our human guests will be arriving shortly, and we can't spoil the surprise too early."

"Right, sorry, I can't see any of the gargoyle's masked forms so it's always fascinating to see other supernaturals as humans. You're stunning, by the way. Good choice. You look like... a model or an actress. Very elegant." Evangeline winces. "Sorry, I talk a lot."

Vara waves her off. "It's fine. Humans usually do when they're nervous, and your heart sounds like it's about to explode in your chest."

Vara locks eyes with Xander.

"Watch this one. I already see a lot of supes looking this way, drooling over her. Especially in that dress."

The gargoyle king growls and bares his fangs.

"No one will touch her," he says.

"I have no doubt about that, King." Vara, chuckles.

"So, *anyway*," Evangeline says, ignoring Xander's protectiveness. "You three really are mates? I couldn't believe it when Xander told me."

Xander gives Thorne an apologetic look. "We don't have secrets. She made me tell her."

Thorne shrugs, amused at his king absolutely simping for the little witch.

Evangeline slaps Xander's chest with the back of her hand. "I didn't make him. He was like a teenage girl with the hot gossip, dying to tell me."

"Kitten, please," Xander says, slightly embarrassed that his mate is revealing his not-so-royal like ways.

"Yes, we are mates," I say with a chuckle.

"But you're not sure how to complete the bond?" Evangeline asks. She immediately grimaces. "Sorry, it's really none of my business."

"It's fine," I say, reassuring the easily embarrassed woman. "We assume it's similar to how gargoyles or vampires mate. Shared pleasure, knotting, and consumption of blood. We just haven't had time to... experiment."

"Xander, my man!" a familiar voice calls out. A cheerful blond fledgling vampire makes his way through the crowd, holding hands with my best friend.

Teddy pushes past me—rude—and releases Millie so he can do one of those bro handshakes with Xander. The way Xander's face lights up with the biggest smile tells me that they've already become fast friends.

"Oh, hey there, Lala," Teddy says, turning to me after the bro-greeting. "I didn't see you there." He pats my head. "So short."

"I will break your hand just so you can be in pain all night while it heals," I say and give him a petty smile.

"Children, behave," Millie butts in, rolling her eyes. She gives me a hug, then walks to Evangeline, giving her one too. "Good to see you again, Evangeline. And you, Xander."

The gargoyle king takes Millie's offered hand and shakes it with a curt nod.

Millie told me she and Teddy met with Xander and Evangeline a few weeks ago. They have a lot in common: both have new mates, and both recently had people connected to them trying to take over control of New York City.

It's one thing we're worried about when it's time to share this unveiling plan with the rest of the supernatural community. There will be many who won't want to be equal to humans and they could retaliate.

Teddy elbows me and when I glance up at him, he waggles his brows. "So, you're getting double stuffed? Tell me you've had both of their tails inside you."

"Not yet, but how delightful does that sound?" Vara says, answering for me.

Teddy groans. "Can Millie and I come over and watch? Or join in?"

Thorne growls beside me, and I squeeze his hand.

"Theodore, go away." I push the horny golden retriever man closer to Millie, and she grabs him by the arm, leading him away with her security team following close behind.

I hear her say something about punishment and roll my eyes.

She's just as horny as him, I swear.

I spot Cyrus and another vampire elder named Zeke on the stage, waving at me to join them.

"I guess it's time," I say and follow my team of bodyguards to the stage with Vara and Thorne beside me.

When I walk onto the platform, Cyrus takes my hand.

"You look marvelous, Queen Aldana."

I murmur my thanks and shift on my feet, suddenly nervous about this next step. The members of SUC were instructed to drop mild hints about the supernatural world with the humans in these high-profile positions that we've befriended. We've been having conversations with them about strange experiences and showing them photos or videos from Vara's clubs. If we found them to be interested or excited, we invited them to tonight's event. If they seemed skeptical in the slightest, appearing to judge us, then we cut ties with them. We didn't compel them or tweak their memories, only because they'll eventually find out, and we're hoping planting that little seed of our existence will help them accept our world when the time comes.

"Thank you, Cyrus," I say, head held high.

He glances behind me.

"How is everything working out with your head of security?"

If I could blush, I would be red in the face right now.

"Amazing. Thorne is perfect. A great protector."

Cyrus narrows his eyes at me. "I'm sure he is... and the sphinx?"

I swallow my suddenly dry throat.

"She's excelling in her position."

Cyrus scoffs.

"Um... her position on the committee, of course."

"Mhm."

I roll my eyes. "It's clear you know about us so just spit it out."

"I know we said unity, but this is not what we meant."

"Yeah, well what's the harm?"

"It's not queen-like!"

"Queen-like? What does that even mean? Human queens and kings throughout history have taken multiple lovers. This is the 21st century. Sex is not dirty. It's natural.

In fact, maybe you should consider a lover with a tail to help remove that stick up your ass."

I smirk and walk past him to the microphone, not waiting for him to tell me it's time to welcome our guests. I hear him mumbling something behind me that I don't care to decipher. I glance at Thorne and Vara who are struggling to hold back their humor. Vara winks at me, and Thorne gives me a thumbs up.

The soft instrumental music that was playing ends and the room falls into silence.

"Thank you all for being here tonight. Everyone in this room is part of a small group who knows about this plan to unveil ourselves to humans. As you know, tonight is our first test. Members of the committee have been working continuously over the past few months to make connections with humans in high-ranking positions. Humans who have sway, who can vouch for us when this plan comes to fruition. Tonight, we reveal ourselves to them and assess the reaction."

Heads nod as the crowd listens.

A young vampire standing at the double doors in the back of the room waves to me, letting me know the humans are ready to enter.

"Without further ado... let's bring them in."

I nod and the doors open.

A group of about three dozen humans walk through, eyes wide and mouths parted in wonder. They hesitate for only a minute before some brave souls move forward. I recognize the tall and slender Black man at the front as a social media influencer. He struts in with confidence, waving at supernaturals he's previously met.

He walks all the way to the front near the stage where he gives me an up and down and a wink. I put my hand on Thorne's forearm when he takes a step forward, growling low enough only I can hear—well, me and a few other supernaturals standing nearby.

Once the room has filled, I motion for the crowd to quiet.

"Welcome to our new guests. You might be confused as to why you're the last ones to arrive. Don't worry, the party has just begun."

Servers are making their way around the room offering drinks and food. The attending supes make sure to grab some to show that it's safe to consume. Not that any of the humans were concerned. Only a few hesitated to grab a glass or a snack.

"So you might ask, what are we celebrating?"

The humans look around the room as if that's where they'll find the answer.

"What if I told you magic was real? Vampires, were-wolves, witches, and every supernatural being you can imagine wasn't make believe?"

A few brows pinch and some raise their voices questioning what the hell they've walked into, but for the most part, excited faces stare back at me. Maybe they think this is some sort of dinner theater. A show... not real.

Well, they're about to see the main event.

"I want to ask you to keep an open mind tonight. What you're about to see may seem impossible. It may frighten you, but I assure you that you are safe here. We welcome all questions you might have, and we'll be happy to answer them."

The crowd quiets in anticipation.

"Are you ready?"

A few people mumble yes. Others are still frozen with worry. I nod to a few witches and vampires who have been assigned to take care of any human who has a bad reaction and help ease their fear with compulsion or a calming spell.

"I'd like for you all to meet the Manhattan Monsters."

One by one, beings that have been masked drop their human appearances—including Thorne and Vara up on stage with me. The vampires in the room show their fangs and the shifters reveal their animal forms. A few screams pierce the quiet air, but it's followed by a chorus of oohs and ahhs and applause. Only three humans have to be escorted out of the room for uncontrollable crying or because they passed out.

"Can't believe your eyes?" I say with a smile. "Don't worry. It's all real. Talk with your neighbors, ask questions."

I leave it at that and exit the stage with Thorne and Vara by my side.

"Well that went better than I expected," Vara says quietly.

"Guess SUC did a great job preparing them," I add.

"Can I just say how much I both love and hate that acronym," Vara adds.

I chuckle and shrug as we weave through the crowd to find the humans we've connected with over the past few months.

"Queen Aldana," a smooth, almost ethereal, voice says from behind me. I turn to find probably the hottest man I've ever seen.

He's a vampire, that's for sure. One I haven't met, which isn't surprising since there are about 2,000 vampires living in New York City. However, this vamp radiates power, and I wonder *why* I don't know him.

He has dark curly hair placed wildly around his head, and his skin is somewhat tanned despite the deathly pallor of being a vampire. His eyes are sapphire blue as I stare up into them, because he's slightly taller than Vara.

She's also drooling over this man and even Thorne can't look away. He must not find the vampire a threat because he hasn't moved to protect us. He did, however, step closer and thread his fingers with mine and Vara's.

"Sorry to interrupt. My name is Rory. I overheard a conversation you were having earlier with the gargoyle king and the short little witch with the protection tattoos."

Is that what those were? I had wondered why the ink had been so vibrant.

"You're in search of someone who knows about three-way mate bonding?"

I nod, my eyes shifting around to make sure no one is paying us attention. All the humans are enthralled with their new supernatural friends, and supes love being the center of attention, so they are focused on the humans, eating up this newfound adoration.

"I can help."

"And you are?" Vara asks, arms crossed and brow raised. She might find him hot, but she doesn't trust him.

"As I said, my name is Rory. But I suppose you might know me as Rorik. Rorik Sevier."

I gasp.

"The first vampire?"

Chapter 17 - Thorne

No fucking way.

"Way," Rorik says, answering my words that I didn't realize I had voiced. I'm confident I *didn't* say them out loud. "I'm intrigued by this unveiling plan. Thought I'd make an appearance to assure you all don't fuck it up."

Vara scoffs, but Layla holds her head up high.

"Well, you see tonight went off without a hitch. Convinced yet?"

The corner of his mouth tilts up slightly, and I wonder how many vampires are brave enough to stand up to him.

"Not yet. Humans are too unpredictable. To be honest, so are we." He tilts his head. "You're not worried, are you, Queen?"

"It's Queen Aldana, *Rory*," Vara hisses. "What kind of name is that anyway for an elder vampire?"

Rorik narrows his eyes at the sphinx. Why is she provoking him?

"I've gone by Rory since I was a child. Sometimes I go by Rorik. You, more than anyone, should know that to survive this long is to adapt. To change with the times. That includes names, *Varalin*."

Vara's eyes widen, and Rory chuckles.

"You think I didn't know your full name? I know every supernatural being in this city." He turns to me. "Even the silent ones."

I blush, which only amuses the vamp.

"Like I said, I can help you three get answers. Unless you don't want to know what happens when you complete the bond."

He turns to walk away.

"No, wait!" Layla says, stepping forward to grab his arm. He looks down as if no one has touched him in decades.

Maybe no one has.

"Of course we'd like your help. I'm sorry about Vara. She can be bitchy sometimes, but you already know that, don't you?"

He glances at Vara, and she snarls at him.

"She's just protecting her mates. She doesn't trust me and that's fair. I can't expect my community to accept me when I've been hiding in the shadows, wallowing in self-pity."

"Old emo ass vampire," Vara mumbles.

Rorik shakes his head at Vara, amused. "Would you three like to set up a time next week to meet?"

"Yes," Layla says, eager with the prospect of getting some answers. "We're all free Thursday night."

Rorik nods. "Then let's do Thursday at midnight."

He reaches out a hand, and Layla accepts it. He gives her a firm shake before offering his hand to me and Vara.

"Now, if you'll excuse me, there are some witches here I'd like to terrorize."

He turns but pauses and pivots back towards us.

"Joking," he says with a wink. "Mostly."

And he walks away chuckling.

"Did that really happen?" Layla asks in awe as if she's just met a celebrity. I suppose for her, she did.

"He's an asshole," Vara grumbles.

"But an asshole with answers," Layla says.

"Okay, let's go dance and socialize so we can get the fuck out of here," Vara says. "Rory got me all riled up and now I'm horny."

Same, to be honest.

The event will go on throughout the night but after another hour of mingling, Layla and Vara have had enough. We make a final round to say our goodbyes, then hop into the SUV to take us back to Layla's penthouse about ten blocks away. We could have walked, but we're more vulnerable that way, even if I've made sure Layla's security team could adequately protect us.

Layla has also expressed how she doesn't want us to fly her around. I think she's a little scared of heights. Hopefully, we can convince her to participate in sky sex at least once.

We make two turns before the team in the SUV behind us notifies me that we're being followed.

I bark at the driver to make an unexpected turn.

"What's going on?" Layla asks from the backseat, panicked.

Before I can explain, the SUV behind us explodes, catapulting us forward. Our SUV lands on its side, glass shattering and metal grinding. My ears ring as I hastily work the seat belt. Supernaturals, especially vampires, quickly learned that heads can be decapitated, and hearts can be impaled when thrown out of a vehicle during a crash. Seat belts are just an extra precaution.

Once undone, I crawl into the back to help Layla and Vara.

"Are you two okay?"

"Yes, I think so," Layla says, her voice shaken.

"I'm fine, but my dress is ruined now," Vara growls, and her humor in this high stress situation somehow eases me.

One of the bodyguards from the SUV that was driving ahead of us appears and helps Vara crawl out through the broken window while I work on Layla's stuck seat belt. Despite my supernatural strength, it's not coming free, so I use the knife from the holster on my ankle and cut her out.

When we emerge on the street, bullets fly.

We fall behind the crashed SUV for protection. I pick up a bullet that fell to the ground after hitting a light pole next to me.

Wooden bullets.

That means whoever is attacking us knows Layla is a vampire. They're trying to assassinate her.

I vaguely register a sharp pain in my side as I grab Layla by the waist.

"Vara, up," I growl, catapulting us into the air.

I fly us above the high-rises, and it takes less than a minute to arrive on the wraparound balcony of Layla's penthouse.

Word of the attack has already reached the security team, and they're outside waiting.

"Lock down the building. Make sure no one enters or leaves. Call William and Finna to help."

Finna is a witch and a new member of the team. She can create a memory spell to help with the human residents in Layla's building who might question what's happening. William is a vampire who can also compel them.

Erebos lands ahead of us.

"Report," I bark.

"Two guards dead, two more injured."

I nod. "Call in a supernatural cleanup team to the street where the SUV explosion and shootout happened so they can help with witnesses and the human first responders."

I turn to another guard, a vampire, waiting for instructions.

"Set up a perimeter two blocks in each direction. Question everyone who tries to cross. This is all hands on deck. Someone was shooting at us using wooden bullets. Everyone needs to wear their armor and activate the protection shields Finna cast."

The vampire nods and leaves.

"Thorne," Layla sobs. "You're bleeding."

One side of Layla's dress is covered in blood where I had her flush against me as I flew us to safety.

I palm her cheek. "I'm fine, Bunny. It will be healed by morning."

I glance behind me, and my stomach drops.

"Where the fuck is Vara?" I ask, panic filling my voice.

"I'm here," she says, landing with a thud. She tosses an unconscious human to the ground. "I spotted the shooter on the roof of one of the buildings we flew over. Thought you'd want to question him."

I approach Vara, and she takes a small step back. I can't imagine the rage she must see exuding from me. If I didn't need the shooter alive, I'd tear his heart from his chest right now.

When I reach the sphinx, I clutch her by the nape and claim her lips. The kiss is quick, possessive.

"You fucking scared us," I growl, resting my forehead on hers.

"Did you forget that sphinxes are guardians too? We know how to fight." She kicks the human on the ground. "This man threatened my mates. I wasn't going to let him get away."

"You think he's a hunter?"

"I assume." Vara kicks him again. Since he's unconscious, there's no reaction.

I wave at one of the other vampire guards still on the balcony with us.

"Take him to the holding cell in the basement. Compel him to tell the truth and report back to me with his answers."

I had the cell installed the first week as Layla's head of security. It has a power suppressor so if any sort of spell has been cast upon the human, it will no longer work in the room.

Vara and Layla are hugging, bloody tears streaming down the vampire's face.

"Thorne," Vara says. "Worry about the human tomorrow. Let him sit in fear for a while and let us see to your wound. Let us take care of you."

I cave, noticing the concern in Layla and Vara's eyes. I give Erebos orders to watch over the human, then let my mates lead me through the balcony's door. I dismiss the soldiers inside, instructing them to take their posts outside the entrance of Layla's penthouse.

The vampire guard who has been staying in one of Layla's guest rooms has long moved out since I'm here every night now.

Layla leads me into the massive en suite bathroom in her bedroom and sits me on the counter. Vara lifts my shirt over my head, the magic-infused fabric separating to clear my wings. Layla is on my other side, and her hands immediately fall to the scars across my chest and stomach.

I suck in a sharp breath when her cold fingertips trace over them. She does this sometimes when we're lying in bed after sex, cuddling. Gargoyles can heal from their wounds, but if the cut is deep enough, scars will be left behind.

"The bullet didn't go through," Vara says, inspecting my wound. "I'll have to dig it out."

"I have a vampire first aid kit," Layla says, turning to the door behind her.

"A vampire first aid kit?" I ask.

"Yeah, once hunters learned to make wooden bullets to kill us, some vampires decided to keep kits on hand in case we got shot and they missed our heart. Wooden bullets make it harder to heal, especially if one is left lodged in our body." She frowns, taking the container out of the closet and handing it to Vara. "I've never had to use it before. I'm so sorry, Thorne."

She leans in, taking my face in her hands and kissing me softly on the lips.

"I would suffer one hundred wooden bullets every day if it meant you'd never feel the pain of just one," I say and kiss her this time, slipping my tongue inside her mouth to lap up her sweet taste.

I moan as her soft lips press against mine. So gentle despite the dangerous vampire I know she can be. So delicate for her large, broody gargoyle mate.

"Done," Vara's voice ends our quick make out session.

The wooden bullet sits on the counter next to me. I didn't even feel her removing it. Guess the pleasure of kissing my mate overruled the pain.

"It's already closing up," Vara says, wiping an alcohol swab over my injury. She washes and dries her hands when finished.

"How are you feeling?" she asks, cupping my neck with her hand.

"I can barely feel the sting anymore. Nothing but a thorn in my side compared to this," I say, pointing at the scar on my face.

"Good," Vara says, a mischievous smile creeping upon her face. "Now, you're going to let Layla and me take care of you for the rest of the night."

She grabs my hand and pulls me off the bathroom counter before I can protest. I'm led into the bedroom with Layla following.

"Finish undressing him," she orders the vampire.

Layla complies, slipping my pants off my body. Again, the magic-infused fabric splits to move past my tail.

"Such a good boy, not wearing underwear for us," Vara purrs.

My cock jumps at her words, pre-cum already dripping from the tip.

"Sit on the bed, wings out," Layla says eagerly.

I do as my queen demands and sit on the end of the bed, allowing plenty of room for my wings to spread out. They're about ten feet from end to end.

"Can we touch them?" Vara asks.

I've never let anyone touch my wings. Not even any of my past lovers. My wings are my lifeline. If they're damaged, they won't heal like the rest of my body. If they receive too many tears, I wouldn't be able to fly.

But for my mates...

"Please," I say, my breathing becoming labored as lust rushes through my body.

The women step on either side of me. Layla is the first to lift her hand. Her fingertips graze over the silk membrane, and I moan in response. Vara places her palm on the stretched, nearly see-through membrane next. My eyes roll into the back of my head, my cock painfully hard and throbbing.

"More," I whimper.

"Tell us what you need, Thorne," Vara says.

Her own wings are out, the golden feathers appear to be vibrating. She's purring with pleasure.

"I need someone to ride me. I'm... I'm about to lose control."

Vara flicks her hand, and Layla jumps into action, undressing quickly and straddling me. She teases me by sliding her slick pussy over my length.

"Fuck, Bunny."

She giggles. I suppose 'fuck bunny' *does* sound ridiculous.

"Get behind him, V," Layla says, and the sphinx complies.

I'm sweating with how much I'm struggling to hold back the need to ravage these two women. I wasn't lying when I told Layla touching my wings would make me feral, but it's clear that they want to be the ones in control tonight.

I'll be submissive for the rest of my life if it makes them happy.

I hiss when Layla wraps her cold fingers around my cock, guiding it to her entrance. Vara settles in behind me, and she grabs my tail. She presses the end to her clit and as if a siren calling to the sea, it starts vibrating. Vara groans.

Layla sinks down on my cock to the hilt, closing her eyes and moaning as her walls stretch around me. She lifts up, then slams back down, causing me to grunt.

"God, I love how vocal you are," Layla says, leaning over to place a kiss on my chest.

Her fangs have dropped, and she scrapes them over one of my scars, hard enough that it draws blood. She licks it up and the cut closes soon after. She then hooks one arm around my neck, allowing her to ride me with ease.

"Are you ready, baby?" she asks. I groan at how tight her wet cunt is as it slides up and down my cock. "I want you to empty everything inside me. Then Vara will drink your cum from my pussy, okay?"

I nod, biting my lip to hold my orgasm at bay until she's ready for me.

Layla's free hand finds my wings, and she slides her palm over the membrane. She's riding me fiercely at this point. Vara is at my back, groaning as the tip of my vibrating tail massages her clit.

Vara's hand presses against the backside of my wing, matching Layla as if the membrane was a glass wall between them.

But their touch and Layla's sweet pussy is too much.

Layla seats herself on my cock the moment I erupt. I scream at how intense it is, my cock pulsing as it pours cum inside her. Once I've let everything out, Vara moves from behind me, and I slide over so she can lie down.

I watch as Layla crawls up her body and hovers over her face. Vara opens her mouth and my warm seed seeps out of Layla and onto Vara's lips. She licks it away like a ravenous dog.

Fuck this is hot.

My cock is already growing hard again.

I move to position myself between Vara's legs. Without warning, I sink inside her. She grabs Layla's thick thighs as I pound her tight heat.

Layla starts riding Vara's face, moaning as Vara covers her clit with her mouth.

It doesn't take long for Layla to shake with her own orgasm. She collapses to the side to let me finish Vara off. She plays with the sphinx's taut nipples while I massage Vara's clit with my thumb.

"So close, Vara," I say. "Your pussy is gripping my cock perfectly."

Layla leans over to take the tip of Vara's breast in her mouth and the moment the vampire bites down over the peak, Vara loses it.

I pump into her a few more times before I, too, reach my second release.

Fuck.

I've never come so much in my life… and we haven't even experienced the ecstasy of completing the bond yet.

Chapter 18 - Layla

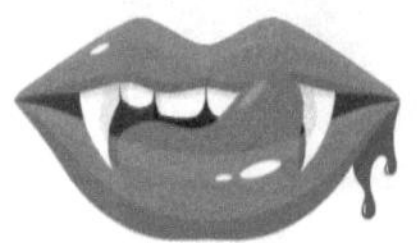

The next week dragged, mostly because Thorne canceled all my public events and refused to let me leave the penthouse after the assassination attempt.

Okay, so he wasn't really holding me prisoner. I could have left anytime, but it was the desperation in his voice that kept me inside—the way he begged me to lay low while investigating who wants to kill me.

I would do anything he asked.

Thorne is concerned about the sudden appearance of human hunters in the city. They rarely come into major cities to kill or capture supes, preferring the suburbs or small towns where supe numbers are smaller... where they're not outnumbered by strong and magical creatures.

Unfortunately, the human we captured was no help. The moment he woke up, and the vampire guard tasked to compel him stepped inside the cell outfitted with the power suppresser, the man started convulsing and foaming at the mouth. Turns out, he had a kill pill inside a fake tooth and bit down on it to avoid having us look inside his head or force him to give us information about the attack.

Thorne believes I'm being targeted because of the unification plan, but it doesn't make sense. Unless one of the new humans we've befriended told someone they weren't supposed to. Like a friend or family member who's a hunter.

While Thorne stayed busy investigating, Vara kept me company. We haven't had much alone time together, not like what I've had with Thorne, so we took advantage of the hours together, fucking, talking, cuddling or watching silly television shows.

The best part was when Thorne would return home and join us on the couch.

I've learned that Vara enjoys reality shows about housewives because they're dramatic. I much prefer competition shows about baking or cooking. When I was human, I was responsible for cooking meals for my husband. I'd become quite good at it, and I enjoyed the time I had to myself. No harsh hands, no cruel words. Just me, food, and a fire to cook it on.

Thorne likes crime documentaries, which I'm not a fan of. Humans are so vile. To think some of them find *us* to be the evil monsters.

Okay, so supernaturals don't have the best track record either, but for the most part, we're no longer dangerous to humans. For many of our kind—like me—we rely on them for sustenance. They don't need to die or be abused for that.

It's now Thursday, just before midnight, and we're heading to the Upper East Side to meet with Rorik.

"So do we complete the bond tonight after Rory explains everything?" I ask, my leg bouncing as we sit in the back of the SUV.

Thorne places his palm on my thigh, and it's as if a shot of calm is jolted throughout my body. I relax against the seat and offer him a thankful sigh.

"I'll have to look at my schedule and move things around, but yes. Why not?" Vara says.

We expect to be out of commission for a month—at least—after completing the bond. It varies. For some supes, it could be days. Others, it might take two months to feel... satisfied. We need to be prepared for however long it takes to solidify our connection.

I squeeze my legs together, thinking about all the fucking we'll be doing. Thorne raises a brow at me, since I've trapped his hand between my legs.

"So eager for us," he whispers before kissing the top of my head.

"I *am* eager. Are you two not?"

"Are you kidding me?" Vara scoffs. "Can you not hear my heart? I'm nervous as hell. How do we know the bond will even work? What if we all have to be in love? I mean, I'm sure I love you both. I definitely like you two a lot."

"So romantic," I tease.

She tosses up her arms, her tail flicking around and nearly hitting me in the eye.

"I just mean... how would the bond know? Would we have to say the words? Would we have to show it somehow with some self-sacrificing deed?"

I burst into giggles, and Vara narrows her eyes at me.

"I'm sorry, am I amusing you?"

I bite my lip attempting to control my fit of laughter. "I love when you're nervous and vulnerable. It makes you seem almost human."

"How dare you. Take it back."

That only makes me laugh harder, and Thorne joins in. I wouldn't say we've lost our minds... I think we're just on edge. The fated mate bond has been gnawing at us...

growing stronger every day we fail to complete it, so every little thing we do is exaggerated.

Like yesterday, Thorne blew his load simply by making out with me.

Our laughter slowly dies just in time for the SUV to pull in front of a building across from Central Park along Fifth Avenue. It's a simple-looking building, about fifteen stories tall, stuck between two other buildings with an off-white brick facade.

Nothing I'd expect the First Vampire to reside in.

Inside, a doorman greets us. He's expecting us and leads us to a private elevator off to the side. He inputs a code into a display and exits. A few seconds later, the doors close, and we're taken to the top floor.

We enter the apartment, which is a duplex. The first room is a sitting or reading area with a single chaise lounge and a fireplace along the green wall. There's a spiral staircase on the opposite side of the room.

"Welcome," Rorik says, suddenly appearing.

Thorne balls his fists at his sides and mumbles something about 'fucking vampire speed.'

Rory scans our group, one of his thick eyebrows rising at the two additional bodyguards Thorne brought with us.

"Would you like a tour?"

"Yes," I say at the same time Vara says, "No."

"Something to drink?"

"No," Thorne and I say at the same time Vara says, "Yes."

Rorik smiles, the expression almost appearing foreign on the face of a vampire known to keep to the shadows.

"Follow me," Rory says, giving me a wink before turning to take us down a hallway.

I push Thorne behind me, knowing he was about to murder Rorik over that harmless wink, and follow the elder vamp. He points out a few bedrooms and a bathroom before we stop in the kitchen. He makes a drink for Vara, not even asking her what she wants. He hands her a glass of vibrant golden booze, and she raises a brow after taking a sip.

"Remy Martin Black Pearl. How did you know this is my favorite?"

Thorne growls, and Vara grabs his hand. "It's okay, Thorne. This vampire is not a threat to you."

He winces. The protectiveness has become worse after the attempted hit on my life. Nearly every day, I've had to calm him down from wanting to rip someone's throat out. I'm pretty sure he would kick someone into an oncoming bus for merely looking at either of us.

"Your nightclubs always have the best liquor," Rory says. "This cognac is the only one you keep on the shelves but don't offer it on the menu."

"Very observant." Vara shrugs. "But it *is* for sale. I only offer it to high-profile supes. If the so-called first vampire had just mentioned his name to any of my bartenders, he would have been served."

"Good to know." He chuckles and turns to lead us into the living space.

It's compact but cozy, the walls in here also green. The vamp loves green, that's for sure. A white couch sits in front of a brick fireplace with two matching white arm chairs on either side. A painting hangs over the fireplace of a vampire fucking what appears to be a human woman who's feasting on a female gargoyle's cunt.

"You like it," he asks me.

It's not a question. He knows I like it because he can smell my arousal. Not to mention my fangs have dropped.

"It's me and my mates," he says.

Our heads slowly turn away from the painting to Rorik who continues to stare at the erotic scene.

"I met them 2,200 years ago when I lived in what is now modern-day Croatia. I was 800 years undead."

"How *did* you become the first vampire?" Vara asks, sitting on the middle cushion of the couch. Thorne and I take a spot on either side of her.

"Ah, yes. You'd like for all the rumors and urban legends to be put to rest. Unfortunately, I can't tell you. I remember waking up with an undying thirst, cold skin, and fangs. No memories of my life before."

He finally looks away from the painting and sits in one of the arm chairs. There's a coffee table between us with a stack of architecture magazines and books about witchcraft.

Interesting mix of reading material.

"Sounds like the work of a witch," I say, pointing at one of his books.

"I thought so too, but I sought their help in those first few years hoping for answers. They tried to reverse what happened to me or to at least ease my thirst. Sadly, nothing worked. Even more unfortunate is killing every single witch who tried to help me. I knew it was wrong, I didn't want to kill them, but the monster inside me was uncontrollable. My thirst was unbearable... unending... I tried to keep my victims alive, but it was too difficult at first. It took about 300 years before I learned to control myself."

"Since you were the first vampire, you obviously created others," I say, fascinated to learn the history of my kind. To fill in the missing pieces of the lore. "How did you figure out the turning process?"

"By my 800th year on this earth, immortality had become quite boring, so... I experimented. It wasn't until I gave my blood to a human on the brink of death that the turn took. I sired my first fledgling. Portia.

"Portia was just as uncontrollable as I had been, maybe worse. She went on to turn dozens of vampires. The undead population was growing too fast, to a point that I killed Portia myself and any other vampire I could find. That's when I met Brynn. She was a gargoyle protecting a small village. She'd heard about me, my reign on humans, and all the new vampires my fledgling had created. Brynn tried to kill me, not caring that I was attempting to right my wrongs."

He smiles at the memory, and my heart clenches. It's clear his mates are no longer alive, and he's still mourning them.

"Gargoyles quickly learned how to kill vampires—by process of elimination or maybe they had witnessed me ripping heads off bodies or tearing hearts from chests. Brynn had me on the ground, a stake to my heart. She sunk it down. Any normal vampire would have turned to dust. Not me. I simply cannot die."

"What?" I gasp, hand to my heart.

Rorik shrugs. "I can walk in the sun as well. I don't understand it, and the witches couldn't figure it out either."

His eyes return to the painting.

"Brynn was confused when I didn't die, she froze while straddling me—as still as stone. Her scent overwhelmed me, honey and vanilla. I couldn't stop my cock from hardening underneath her. She snapped out of her shock that I hadn't died, fury battling with her lust. She was the first to make a move, pulling my cock from my pants and riding me while using the knife's handle—still embedded in my chest—like the horn of a saddle."

Okay... that sounds hot as fuck.

"It *was* hot," Rory says, seemingly echoing my thoughts. "We spent several days together, but I needed to feed. That's when I met a human named Eden. A beautiful, curvy little thing. Her blood smelled magnificent. Nothing like I ever tasted before. I nearly drained her of every last drop, but Brynn was there to stop me. Brynn could sense that this human was different."

"Fascinating," Vara whispers. "A human, a vampire, and a gargoyle. So how did you complete the bond?"

"We had no idea we were fated mates at the time. Brynn knew soulmates existed for gargoyles and other creatures, but cross-species soulmates? It was unheard of. So, we didn't know a bond needed to be completed. We just knew we were always horny for each other. Always needing to be near each other. Always needing to protect one another.

"Bonding happened by accident. We were having a lot of sex and one night, maybe a month after we found each other, the three of us reached orgasm at the same time while feeding off each other. A bright light filled the room, and we all passed out."

"So, it's not any different from vampires completing their bonds," I say.

"And gargoyles," Thorne adds.

"I *assume* it will be a similar experience for you three. Remember, I had a human for a mate, not a sphinx." Rorik says and gestures to Thorne. "And with you being a male gargoyle, knotting will likely need to be involved. Just know your orgasms and feeding off each other have to be exact. Not a second off."

He narrows his eyes at us.

"The bond desperately wants to be completed. I'm surprised you didn't think of shared orgasms and feeding before now."

I wince. "Well, we suspected this was the way it was done, but Vara and I have been busy with the Supernatural Unveiling Committee. We had events and meetings to attend, and we didn't have weeks or months to dedicate to the so-called hibernation period that comes after bonding."

"Speaking of..." Vara says, leaning forward slightly. "How long did it take for the bond to strengthen?"

"We spent nearly five weeks in bed, emerging only because I turned my human mate, and we needed to find her someone to feed off of."

"What about other things?" I ask. "Like my friend Millie. After she bonded with her blood mate, she was able to withstand the sun, and her tears no longer bled."

"Yes, all those things happened with Eden. She was also highly desirable to other supernatural beings. I believe that only applies to humans who are destined to be a vampire's mate. Something in their blood makes it more potent."

Okay, so I don't have to worry about that happening to Vara and Thorne. They're my mates but not technically blood mates.

"As for me, nothing changed. My tears still bleed, my heart does not beat, and I'm still able to walk in the sun as I always have. Brynn also did not experience any outrageous changes. However, you'll be able to sense where your mates are at all times. You will know when they're in danger. Your thoughts can be shared."

"So, what's the purpose?" Vara asks. She winces at how hostile the words sounded. "I just mean why, after all these years, did we find each other now? Layla and Thorne are both over 700 years old. I've always sensed my mates, but why did it take so long to find them?"

Rorik shrugs, spreading his palms open in front of him.

"There might not be a reason. Or there is something bigger on the horizon. You very well know that supernatural beings are stronger with a mate."

Vara frowns, and Thorne places his palm on her thigh. Her tense shoulders sag slightly at his touch. Her tail, however, doesn't calm down, and it jerks around beside her.

"I'm sorry I do not have better answers. But think about the day you met." Rorik looks at Vara. "And I'm not talking about the brief meeting at your club with Layla."

What the fuck? How did he know? Was he watching from the shadows? Does he have spies?

"What was happening the first time the three of you were in the same room?"

"I held a ball, and Thorne agreed to be my head of security. The Supernatural Unveiling Plan was coming to fruition," I whisper.

"You think something's going to happen?" Thorne asks, his wings unlatching from his back. It happens anytime he senses danger or the urge to defend us, as if preparing for takeoff... preparing to attack.

Rorik shakes his head. "I've sought a few seers to ask that very question. Unfortunately, there are too many unknown variables. They've seen war, but they've also seen a unified world between humans and supes. Whatever the outcome, I believe that this unveiling plan is why destiny brought you three together. The reason could be as simple as protecting each other if it comes down to war. Or maybe it's just to provide each other pleasure and happiness in this new life."

Rorik's watch beeps, and he sighs.

"I'm afraid I must go. Let me walk you out."

When we get to the door, I turn to the elder vamp. "What happened to your mates?"

He smiles sadly. "I had one hundred glorious years with them."

It's all he says, and I don't push the topic. It's clear he's still mourning them, even after all these years. I can't imagine how he was able to live on after losing two pieces of his heart. How painful it must have been.

Which is why we must complete the bond tonight, because destiny brought us together for a reason, and I'm not about to tempt fate.

Chapter 19 - Vara

Our meeting with Rory was a waste of time.

We already suspected how to activate the fated mate bond. Not to mention the emo fucker had no additional insight into why we found each other now instead of hundreds of years earlier. I had already told Thorne and Layla that I believed it's because of the unveiling plan.

"What's wrong, V?" Layla asks, pouting. "Why's my sphinxy so mad?"

I blanch. "First of all, never call me sphinxy again. Second of all, we didn't need Rory's help. All we learned was he's a sad little creep."

"He was kinda creepy," Layla says, scrunching her nose. "How did he know about the first time we met?"

"I don't know or care to find out."

"I'm pretty sure he can read minds," Thorne offers. "At the unity event last week, I had a thought, and he verbally answered it. I know I didn't say it out loud."

"Then he's a creep for listening to our thoughts without our consent," I say. "The point is, he knew nothing."

Thorne shrugs. "He validated your theories though."

I wave off his words.

"Oh, V." Layla tsks, and I stifle the urge to roll my eyes. "So moody. What can we do to make you feel better?"

The SUV pulls up to her building since it's closer than my place. She grabs my hand, and we exit the car, but instead of walking through the front doors, Thorne takes hold of me and Layla by the waist and shoots us up into the air.

Layla shrieks and buries her head into Thorne's chest while I punch the gargoyle in the stomach. He pretends it hurts and chuckles, but his grip on me doesn't loosen. Within seconds we land on Layla's balcony, and I push him away.

"I have wings of my own, you know."

He must have called or texted one of the guards because they're at the door, unlocking it for us.

"If you hated it so much," he begins, that stupid adorable grin on his face, "then why are you smiling?"

"I'm only smiling at the thought of me kicking you in the nuts if you ever do that again."

"I'd rather you cradle my nuts while I fuck your mouth."

He gives me a peck on the lips, then walks into Layla's penthouse. Layla appears at my side and leans her head on my arm.

"He's adorable, isn't he?"

I scoff. "Fortunately, I adore the fucker, otherwise, he'd be dead for flying off with me without my consent."

"Come on, my mate," Layla says.

My mate.

The words fill my chest with an unnerving feeling of joy. I'm still not used to it. Maybe that's why I'm so angry. My entire life of loneliness and relying on myself is about to end. My soul is about to be shared with two other beings. What if they get sick of me? What if they realize this is a mistake? I can't have them breaking my heart after I hand it over in pieces. I'll never be able to put it back together again.

When I walk into the penthouse behind Layla, her hand never leaving mine as she leads me to the bedroom, all my doubts fade.

Thorne stands next to the bed, his shirt already off. Scars mar his chest and stomach, and I chastise myself for being so selfish. I'm not the only one making sacrifices. We all are. Thorne watched his family get murdered by hunters. He's been hesitant to love because of that. Layla spent her human life being owned by a man who abused her. She killed her sire for trying to control her like her wretched husband. She was scared of love because of that abuse, but she's here now, ready to give part of her soul to us.

They are *both* here with me now. They are just as vulnerable as I am.

Thorne holds out his hands: one for me, one for Layla. I take it and a zing of electricity shoots through my body. Layla whimpers, feeling it too.

It's as if our bodies know it's happening.

Thorne tugs until we're both flush with his body, his arms sliding around our waists, so he's sandwiched between us. Leaning down, he kisses Layla first. I swear I can feel the ghost of his mouth on my own lips. He kisses me next, and it's both soft and *eager*.

"My mates," he says when we part, a goofy smile lighting up his face.

"We should discuss logistics," I say, nearly out of breath from the kiss. My pleasure is already soaking my inner thighs.

"Logistics?" Layla snorts. "How sexy."

"I'm serious," I say.

Layla pats my shoulder. "I know, babe."

The vampire is being a brat, so I reach out and fist her shirt, then push her onto the bed face first. She yelps at the sudden move and squirms when I peel off her pants and underwear.

"Spank her, Thorne."

He doesn't hesitate and the crack of his hand falling on her ass cheek echoes throughout the room.

"Fuck!" Layla screams out.

I start undressing, slipping off the sheer fabric of my halter top and mini skirt. Thorne spanks Layla again and again until welts form. They disappear fast because of her vampire healing.

"Now eat her ass," I order.

I crawl into the center of the bed, sitting on my knees to watch the gargoyle spread Layla's plump cheeks apart and bury his face between them. His wings are fully extended, and they shudder the moment his long, thick tongue pokes past the tight ring of muscle.

Layla jerks, her hands fist the comforter, and she whimpers because Thorne isn't being gentle. He's fucking her asshole with that talented tongue, fast and furious like the good boy that he is.

I clutch Layla's chin.

"Open those pretty lips."

When she does, I spit in her mouth.

"Good girl," I whisper, giving her a kiss. "Now come for Thorne."

Thorne's tail slips underneath Layla, finding her clit. It presses against the sensitive bundle of nerves and vibrates. Layla screams and buries her face into the bedding as her body convulses. I moan too, her pleasure spreading through me. It's strong enough that I nearly come.

Thorne stands and licks his lips. His bulbous cock is rock hard and straining against the seam of his pants.

I grab Layla by the hair and lift her head.

"You and Thorne undress each other, then I want you to crawl on top of me."

Layla nods, and I get into position while my mates undress. They're eager, so within seconds, they're naked and ready.

"Do you have instructions for us?" Layla asks, a brow quirked. She's being sassy with me.

"As a matter of fact, I do. Thorne's going to fuck that tight pussy of yours from behind while you're on top of me, that way he can knot. His tail will take me in the ass. When we come together, Layla will bite down on my breast, I will drink from Thorne's wrist, and Thorne can sink his fangs into Layla's neck."

"So sexy," Layla teases.

"Get the fuck over here," I growl and Layla giggles. The sound is lovely, like a song performed by the world's greatest symphony. If I were to never hear her laugh again, I fear I would forget how to breathe and simply die.

"You will not die," Layla says, rolling her eyes.

"You heard that?" I ask, eyes wide.

"You didn't say it out loud," Thorne answers. "We heard it though. The bond is anxious if we can hear each other's thoughts so clearly now."

Layla slowly crawls up my body. I take her by the throat, bringing her face to mine, and crush my lips to hers. Thorne doesn't waste time. He's behind Layla, and she gasps when he slides the tip of his cock up and down her slit.

"Let him stretch you, Bug."

Layla straddles my hips, her front nearly smashed to mine. Her fangs have dropped, her eyes solid black. I squeeze her throat and kiss her again, drowning out her scream when Thorne thrusts inside her.

His tail teases my ass, the tip self-lubricating to prepare me. Once satisfied, it transforms into a phallic shape and slides into me with ease.

"Yes," I moan as he pounds into Layla viciously to match the pumps of his tail.

My wings have spread open, so have Thorne's, and he uses the ends to slip between our bodies and tease our nipples. I slide my hand down to reach Layla's clit, and she has the same idea, finding mine and pressing her finger down to massage it.

"Oh, fuck, Thorne," Layla screams. "Your cock is growing."

It's preparing to knot.

"I can't last much longer," he groans.

I expected the bonding ritual to be quick as our souls are more than ready to be bound.

Thorne grunts as he drives into Layla, his tail matching the jerk of his hips. He leans over, his lips brushing the nook of the vampire's neck. His fangs scrape against the skin. He holds out his arm for me to take.

"Are you ready?" I ask them.

"Y-yes," Layla wheezes.

"Now," Thorne growls, and he stills when his knot expands enough that he's no longer able to move while inside Layla.

The tip of his tail also expands in *me*. When it starts vibrating, I'm sent over the edge at the same time Thorne moans and Layla screams. My fangs have already sunk into Thorne's wrist. Layla's drinking from the peak of my breast, and Thorne is latched onto Layla's neck.

I don't know how we made this work. I'm sure we resemble a pretzel. But the moment a bright light bursts throughout the room and my vision starts to fade, I know we did it.

We completed the bond.

Chapter 20 - Thorne

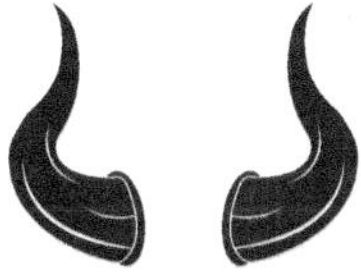

Amonth and a half.

That's how long it took to strengthen and satisfy the bond.

It was more than just sex. We also cuddled while talking about our long lives, the places we lived, and the things we still want to do. Like Layla, who wants to go to Disney World because she's never been. Vara who wants to open her first human/supernatural club once we reveal ourselves to their world.

And me.

I want to write a mystery book.

They're small aspirations, but new experiences for all of us, which is rare for our kind.

Spending the past month and a half with Layla and Vara, with no responsibilities for once in my life, was nice. The timing was perfect since we still have no leads on the human who shot at us with wooden bullets. There haven't been any additional attacks, which isn't surprising since Layla hasn't been out in public, except for the meeting with Rorik.

I canceled Vara and Layla's in-person appearances, so all their meetings were done virtually, including the bi-weekly meeting for SUC. No one questioned Layla and Vara appearing together on video. Except for Locheran, who they ignored.

Not that it mattered. Supernaturals are horrible gossips so word got out fast that Layla, Vara, and I are mates. We had to report our relationship to WOVE who gave Layla reprieve for the bondymoon. That's what Layla called the honeymoon for completing the bond.

It's now two weeks until the International Supernatural Conference. Tonight's in-person SUC meeting will involve going over the itinerary for the event. There will be guest speakers, humans and supernaturals alike. Video presentations showing unity amongst our kind and even a few videos of humans and supes working together. Locheran also formed an inter-species special ops team to focus on stopping self-proclaimed monster hunters. That team will have their own presentation at the conference.

One day will solely be for hearing concerns from the supernatural community.

For the most part, we're prepared. Yet the pit in my stomach grows deeper every day.

Vara pouts as we pile into the SUV, Layla between us. My first in command, Erebos, is in the front seat with the driver. I left the griffin in charge while I was on my 'bondy-moon' but since we've emerged from the sex cave—Layla's words, not mine—I'm back in the lead role. With tonight being our first public appearance in nearly two months, I beefed up security. One vehicle leads us to the WOVE building in Lower Manhattan while two others follow.

"I don't want to go to work," Vara whines.

Layla laughs, taking the sphinx's paw in her hand. She kisses her knuckles. "We'll have plenty of time to play after this conference is over."

I hope.

Those unspoken words silence us. The truth is, we have no idea if this plan will work. If it doesn't, we go to war and one of us could die.

All of us could die.

"Everything's going to work out," Layla says, hearing my thoughts. I've been working on putting up walls to keep them in, but sometimes I forget.

Layla takes my hand and brings it up to kiss my knuckles just as she had done with Vara. My tense body relaxes slightly at her touch. Desire takes over, and I grab my mate by the throat so I can claim her lips.

It doesn't matter how much the three of us have fucked, we will always want more. I've released enough cum to fill a lake at this point. Yet just the brush of Layla's mouth, a graze of her fingertips over my skin, has me hard and leaking.

We spend the rest of the drive giving in to our lust, making sure to be careful about simultaneous orgasms. Rorik said it could take years for the passing out part to lessen.

Everyone is already seated when we walk into the conference room. Layla takes her place at the front and Vara sits next to Locheran. He raises a brow at her, and she flips him off. I snort and pull out my phone when it vibrates in my pocket.

Sex looks good on you, brother.

Loch

My chest puffs out, my heart fluttering.

Brother.

I've been helping Locheran with the security aspects of the unveiling plan as well as the protocols for the upcoming conference. There were plenty of nights during our bondymoon where he'd come over with Xander and Evangeline and the six of us would eat and/or drink and talk about the adventures we've had in our long lives... well except for Evangeline since she's only lived forty human years.

They've all become my family.

Now we just need Locheran to find *his* mate. I can tell he's lonely. He might joke and be an asshole, but I've known him long enough now to understand that's his way of coping. He's even told me that he believes he'll be alone for the rest of his life. He claims he's fine with random hookups, but his eyes contradict his words.

I text him back a middle finger emoji, which makes him chuckle. Then I follow it up with a 'thank you.'

The meeting lasts nearly two hours as we go over the itinerary and security details. When we leave the building, we're exhausted and ready for cuddles and a movie. But the moment we step outside, I sense something's wrong.

We're being watched.

I hold out my arms to stop Vara and Layla from walking forward. Erebos walks to our SUV and finds a letter on the windshield. I turn to the guards tasked with monitoring activity around the building.

"How did this get here?" Erebos asks, angrily. I can always count on him to take his job seriously and do it well.

Their mouths flap open and closed like a fish out of water.

"It wasn't there a minute ago," a vampire guard says. "I just did a sweep."

Erebos brings the letter to me. "It could have been any supe with magical abilities. Anyone with speed or a cloaking power."

I snarl at the thought of a supe with malicious intents getting close enough without being seen.

The paper isn't much of a letter at all. It contains only one sentence:

Cancel the conference or many will die.

Goddamn it.

As I pass the paper to Layla and Vara to read, the SUV that we were seconds from entering explodes. The blast sends the three of us backwards. Erebos lands next to me, but he's quick to get back on his feet. He extends his wings, taking to the air to scope out a possible suspect.

But whoever placed the letter is long gone.

I scramble to find Layla and Vara. They were thrown a few feet away from me. Aside from a few scrapes—that are already healing—and their skin covered in ash from the fire and smoke, they're uninjured. The panic building inside me fades knowing they're alive.

Erebos lands back next to me. "Two guards are injured, a vampire and a shifter. I hear sirens off in the distance, so someone already called human first responders."

I nod and instruct him to call a supernatural clean up team to compel and alter memories.

We're going to need them.

"We should cancel the conference," I growl.

I stand in Layla's penthouse living room, arms crossed.

It's been a week since another attempt to kill Layla was made. At least, we assume it's Layla being targeted. For all we know, it could be Vara.

I considered myself, then concluded that I barely have friends, let alone enemies. Everyone from my past is dead, including the hunters who took my family away from me.

The news of the explosion spread fast amongst our kind and supes are getting nervous. The hunters are getting bolder in their attacks, using bombs in a crowded city where other humans could be injured or killed.

Xander has all hands on deck, trying to find the humans before there's another incident.

"No. Absolutely not," Layla says, pacing in front of me. Vara sits on the couch, legs crossed and appearing bored as she preens her feathers and sharpens her claws. "It's what they want. I will not let them have their way. We've worked too hard for this. If someone wants to kill me, they'll find a way. I won't sit here waiting for them to attack. The conference will be secure and if they try to kill me there, they won't succeed. You or Locheran will catch them."

Supernatural Crime Investigators scoured the burnt-out SUV and watched surveillance footage from surrounding buildings but found nothing useful. SCI said it's likely the bomb was installed hours earlier. Possibly even days. It could have happened when the SUV was parked while the driver got gas, or took a break, or parked it for the night in the garage at Layla's building.

We checked the cameras in the basement parking garage too but didn't find any movement to suggest a bomb was being attached to the SUV. The only thing the investigators noticed was a slight glitch when the letter was being put on the windshield.

It could have been a witch or any other supernatural with cloaking abilities. Whoever it is knows about the supernatural conference since they threatened more deaths if the event proceeds. We're wondering if a supe who knows about the unveiling plan, and is against it, is behind the attacks. If that's the case, someone on the committee, or any supe that was invited to the unity event with humans, has been talking.

We've questioned the SUC members already, but they all denied leaking the sensitive information. Not that they'd admit it if they were, but Vara and I are both good at detecting lies and they all seemed genuinely concerned. We've tasked them with keeping an ear out amongst their species for any word of discourse over the plan.

It was inevitable that word got out before our announcement at the conference. There are rarely secrets with supernaturals.

The only thing that doesn't make sense is the human shooting at us. We assumed he's a hunter, but maybe he's not. Maybe he's working with supes to make sure this unification plan doesn't happen.

"Then reschedule it for another date." I continue my plea with Layla. "Let me find this asshole first and once the danger is over, the conference can go on."

Layla pinches the bridge of her nose as if my insistence on protecting her is giving her a headache.

She's definitely being a pain in my ass.

Vara snorts.

Fucking mate thoughts.

"Thorne, look. The only reason you're freaking out about this is because I'm your mate. Trust me, I'm scared something will happen to you and Vara as well. But isn't this why we were brought together?"

"We don't know that," I growl.

Layla crosses the room in seconds, her hand striking out like a snake to take me by the neck. "First of all," she says, using the couch as a stepping stool to hover her mouth over mine, "don't fucking talk to me like that."

She licks my lips, and I whimper.

Fucking bond always making me horny.

Vara snorts... again.

Glad she finds this entertaining.

"Oh, I am definitely entertained. I would love to see Layla hand you your ass," Vara says, not even looking at us as she flips through a celebrity gossip magazine now that she's done grooming herself.

Layla's fangs drop, and she grazes them over my cheek and chin while still squeezing my neck.

"Second of all, my mate," Layla says, licking up the blood from the cut she just made. "I am the vampire queen of New York City. I will not submit to those who want me to fail. I will get on that stage during the conference in a week and make it clear that anyone who revolts because of this unveiling plan, anyone who causes harm to humans and/or supes, will be punished by death."

She releases me, and I adjust my painfully hard cock. There's no way I'll be getting any relief tonight after the way I raised my voice at my mate.

Layla collapses onto the couch next to Vara with an exaggerated sigh. "It's clear this person doesn't understand the hard work we've put into this plan. We're not going to implement it unless the majority of our community is on board. It's why we're holding public hearings for supes to weigh in. They resorted to violence when all they had to do was come to us to raise their concern."

"Maybe the attacks have nothing to do with SUP," I offer.

"God, I hate that acronym too," Vara laughs. "Who came up with it?"

Layla ignores Vara and holds out her hand for me. I join her on the couch, and she cuddles up to my side.

"I trust you and Locheran will find who's responsible. I will be fine, I promise. I know it's your job to protect me, but you do realize I was a warrior before I was a queen, right?"

I nod.

"I fought in armies against vampire hunters and ripped their throats out with my fangs. I can take care of myself. This security team I've been assigned is merely a formality as queen."

I wrap my arm around her shoulders and rub her arm.

"I know you can take care of yourself, but don't get cocky on me. You know very well there are other supes stronger and more powerful than you."

Chapter 21 - Layla

The past week went by quickly as SUC made final preparations for the conference. There weren't any more attempted attacks, no more cryptic letters or even suspicious beings hanging around.

Thorne is convinced their next target is tonight at the opening of the International Supernatural Conference.

I don't doubt it either.

Vara walks out of her massive closet in a sleek red dress with thin straps and a neckline that dips all the way down to her navel. The fabric falls over the curves of her hips like liquid. She turns to give herself a once-over in the mirror and my fangs drop.

Fuck.

Her ass is so juicy, I want to bite *it.*

"Patience, Lollipop. You can bite my ass when we get home tonight."

I've rather enjoyed the shared thoughts part of the bond. Mostly because Thorne blushes anytime he hears me think about him or Vara... those thoughts are never innocent either.

She flutters her wings behind her and adjusts the headdress she's wearing—it has matching red diamonds and gold spikes banding around her skull—and she fluffs her blonde hair styled in a braid that hangs over her shoulder.

I want to fist my hands in the mane while she has her nose buried in my—

She turns to me with a heated smile.

"Behave yourself, Queen. We're already running late, and I can't fuck you in the car on the drive to the venue either. I will *not* have an entire room of supes smelling that sweet cunt after I make you come all over my fingers."

She moves me toward the mirror.

"Beautiful," she says, skimming her palms over my arms.

Tonight's attire isn't meant to be formal, but Vara wears whatever she wants. For me, I went with a black jumpsuit with short sleeves and a gold belt around the high waistline. My hair is down in soft curls around my face. Vara broadcasts an image of Thorne wrapping the locks around his wrist while she orders him to fuck me.

Wow. We're all horny as fuck.

Vara presses her soft lips to my shoulder, then grabs her clutch and offers me an arm. "Ready?"

We walk out of her bedroom and find Thorne standing before a few of my security team members, going over procedures for tonight. I'm sure they've heard them about a million times already.

When a few of the guys on the team widen their eyes, spotting Vara and me walking into the room, Thorne stops talking and turns to face us.

"Out," he growls, and the team doesn't think twice, filing out the front door.

"Our gargoyle guard is so jealous, isn't he, Layla?" Vara purrs, taking Thorne's face and placing a gentle kiss on his lips. She doesn't linger, making sure not to mess up her lipstick.

"I will be struggling all night trying not to stab out the eyes of every creature that looks at you two."

Thorne kisses me softly, careful not to smear my lipstick either.

"You two look absolutely stunning," he says and with his arms around our waists, he leads us out the door.

The drive from Lower Manhattan into Brooklyn where the conference is being held takes nearly thirty minutes because of Friday night traffic.

We pull up to a back entrance of the arena in Prospect Heights. The door opens and we exit to a team of bodyguards waiting to escort us in. Thorne is behind us as Erebos leads.

We weave through hallways that are meant for staff until coming upon a holding area where speakers for tonight will gather before going up on stage. Thorne veers off to talk to Locheran about security measures and leaves Erebos to wait with us.

Cyrus and a team of vampire elders emerge from a hallway that house a few conference rooms.

"Queen Aldana," he says, approaching and offering a slight bow.

It's such a formal greeting from a man who months ago criticized me for fucking two beings at the same time.

Vara growls beside me, obviously hearing my thoughts.

I forgot about that. Let me kill him, she thinks back to me.

Before I can tell her to forget about the prudish elder, Thorne returns to my side.

Cyrus narrows his eyes at the gargoyle, and Thorne bares his fangs in return. The elder vamp quickly looks away.

Coward.

"Any issues?" I ask Thorne, ignoring the elder vamp. He gasps at the dismissal, turning on his heel and stomping off.

Fucking baby.

Thorne leads Vara and me away to a corner. "No. It's quiet. Too quiet. I don't like it."

"Queen Aldana," a production assistant for the conference says, approaching us with a tablet.

Vara and Thorne both give her a look that causes her to stumble back slightly. She's a young fae, possibly fifty years in age, who hasn't quite come into her powers, whatever they might be. The tips of her pointed ears redden, and she lets out a small puff of air.

"Ignore them," I say, stepping closer to the woman. "What is it?"

"The room is at capacity. They'd like you to start early."

"No," Thorne growls.

"Okay. Give me two minutes, and I'll head out."

The fae nods and nearly runs off.

"This is when they'll attack. They're changing the schedule to throw us off," Thorne says.

"Sounds like you've already figured out their diversion so you can intervene." I place my hand over his heart, which thrashes violently against his chest. "I guarantee that scared fae girl is just doing her job. She's not part of some elaborate attack plan."

"You don't know that."

"Fine, I don't, but it doesn't matter because you're ready. We're ready."

I lift on the tips of my toes so I can cup his cheek, and his eyes close at my touch. My heart responds with a single beat. Ever since we completed the bond, it's been slowly coming back to life. The first time I felt it beat, I cried. My tears are no longer bloody either, more of a light pink, which made me cry even harder.

And the sun.

While I no longer burst into flames during daylight, the sun still burns my skin. I'm hoping that will lessen over the years. Thorne was curious, too, and he stepped out underneath the bright sky.

He experienced something similar. He didn't turn to stone immediately, but his velvet skin started to harden after half an hour.

"I love you, Thorne."

His eyes widen, because technically, it's the first time I've said it to him. He leans down and gives me a quick peck. His mouth lingers, tickling my lips as if debating whether to mess up my lipstick with a devouring kiss. Instead, he pulls back with a goofy smile.

"I love you too."

I turn to Vara.

"I love you, my sphinxy pie."

"Absolutely not. Remove that from your vocabulary immediately." She laughs, despite her disgust with the nickname, then her face softens because it's also the first time I've said those three little words to her. "And I love you. More than life itself."

"So dramatic," I say with a giggle because I wouldn't have her any other way.

Vara doesn't do simple. She keeps her emotions to herself, only allowing Thorne and me to see her compassionate side. For her to say such a vulnerable thing, especially in public, has my heart beating twice in a row.

Vara's kiss is more consuming and when she releases me, she licks her thumb and fixes my smudged lipstick.

With a wink, she sends me off.

I walk to the stage and wait in the wings for the announcer to welcome the guests and introduce me as the first speaker of the night. When my name is called, the crowd erupts in cheers. I might have heard a few boos, but I push that out of my mind and lift my head high as I head to the center of the stage.

"Esteemed guests, thank you for joining us on this first night of the International Supernatural Conference."

I pause for cheers and glance to the side of the stage at Thorne. He meticulously scans the crowd for threats. I know Locheran and his security team are doing the same at different vantage points around the room, which is packed with hundreds of supes.

When the applause subsides, I continue.

"This is my first time at the conference in my new role as vampire queen of New York City, and I have been hard at work on a huge project. One that might seem terrifying, but I truly believe it will benefit us in the long run."

A few heads turn and chatter arises as the supes in the room question what I'm talking about.

"Now, I want you to have an open mind tonight and the rest of this weekend. This is only a plan and plans can change. We want input from you before anything is finalized." I turn to welcome my guest to the stage. "I'd like to introduce you to Senator Virginia Faraday from New York."

The noise in the room rises and a few supes take a fight-ing stance, ready to protect themselves and those around them as the human walks out onto the stage and stops beside me.

"Please," I say, raising my voice above the chatter. "Senator Faraday knows of our kind. She is an ally."

Shocked faces stare back at me. A few angry ones too, but mostly curious ones leaning forward, eager for me to continue. The senator is the first human to attend a supernatural conference. Even human mates are not allowed.

"For the past eight months, I've been leading a committee for a supernatural unveiling plan. Our members have been making human connections and gauging their reaction to our existence. Senator Faraday is one of those humans who will be advocating for protections for our kind.

"This weekend, we will be hosting panels where we discuss the unveiling plan. We'll hold public forums so you can voice your concerns and ask questions. This is not something we will do if the majority of our community is against it. But we believe the time to emerge from the shadows is now. With technology advancing, it's only a matter of time before our kind is discovered, and we'd rather be the ones in control of that discovery."

A few mumbles of agreement wash over the crowd.

"I know one of the main concerns is the rise in hunter attacks on supes. That's where Senator Faraday can help."

I nod and switch places with her. The human isn't intimidated at all. She holds her head high, looking every bit a politician with her perfectly shaped bun at the nape of her neck, and her black pants suit with a dark blue blouse underneath.

"Thank you, Queen Aldana. I've been working with the queen and other committee members about the safety concerns involving the unveiling. I promise to work with my colleagues in Washington to make sure laws are passed, one's that would deem it illegal to harm a supernatural being unless it is in self-defense. This will also protect supernatural beings who rely on humans for life sustenance like the vampires. Layla has informed me they already have rules in place that require consent for blood donations. Similar rules will need to be implemented so humans are protected as well. We must reassure humans and supernaturals alike that we are of no harm to each other.

"I know there are also concerns that supes will be captured and experimented on. That will be another piece of legislation I construct. Humans will be banned from nonconsensual testing on supernaturals. However, you are welcome to offer yourself for testing voluntarily or for a fee. I look forward to speaking with you all this weekend. I will be around at every panel, every forum, to answer your questions and hear your concerns. Thank you."

She steps away, and I return to the microphone.

"I know that there will always be bad apples amongst our kind, but there are bad humans as well. Humans have laws as we do, but if we move forward with an unveiling plan, then our laws will combine with theirs."

A low hum falls within the crowd as people turn to their neighbors to discuss and process the announcement.

"Now... over the next hour we'll have more guests, both humans and supernaturals, to talk about the unity plan. I'll be back soon for more discussions and announcements and later tonight, there will be a human/supe mixer. Thank you for your time."

The conference host returns and thanks me and Senator Faraday.

When we're out of view from the crowd, I shake hands with the politician, and she's escorted away with her own security team to a green room somewhere in the back.

I turn to find Thorne standing next to me.

"I think that went well!"

He leans down and kisses my forehead. "You were amazing."

"And no attack!" I glance around him. "Where's Vara?"

"What do you mean? She was just..."

His voice trails off when he realizes our mate is no longer standing behind him.

Chapter 22 - Vara

I'm fucking pissed.

Kidnapped!

Unbelievable.

One moment I'm standing behind Thorne as Layla shakes hands with the motherly looking senator woman, and the next, I'm lifted off the ground and something is injected into my neck.

I passed out seconds later.

Honestly, though. Kidnapped?

How original. Millie's blond human—now vampire—mate was kidnapped by a feral vampire. Evangeline was kidnapped by Xander's psychotic brother.

Do villains not have any other way to deliver their message?

"You can scowl all you want, but it won't save your life."

I woke up about five minutes ago in a nondescript room, no windows, tied to a chair with a human man sitting across from me. His cheeks flare red, his hair thinning on top of his head, and he's got a little bit of a belly hanging over his belt.

I'll call him Frank because he looks like a Frank.

Next to Frank is Erebos in his human form.

Fucking traitor.

How did no one see him take me? Guards were everywhere!

Despite my supernatural strength, the ropes are too tight, and I can't escape. It's also possible they're infused with a spell that's preventing me from tearing the material. Or whatever I was injected with is suppressing my abilities.

"I thought sphinx were supposed to be strong?" Frank asks. "No... you're supposed to be smart, right? Give me a riddle. I want to see if I can solve it."

The human has an accent. Russian possibly. He chuckles at his abysmal attempt at humor.

I scoff.

Sure, sphinxes were known to use riddles to protect tombs and treasures. Anyone who failed to solve it was killed. Anyone who solved the riddle got to kill the sphinx and access the riches—which never happened.

I always hated coming up with riddles. I would have rather battled with my body than my mind. Though as I got older, I realized I was meant for leadership roles not ones meant for a warrior.

My parents and siblings loved coming up with riddles. They were so smart and creative. I suppose that's why I was only ever given one assignment.

"When I get out of these ropes, I will rip your heart out of your asshole and stuff it down your throat just so I can tear it out of your anus for a second time," I seethe.

"Well, that's a shitty riddle," Frank mumbles.

"It's called a threat, you imbecile." I turn to Erebos. "Why? What's in it for you?"

He shrugs. "Money."

I roll my eyes.

Griffins are known to spend money, either on extravagant vacations, gambling, or buying useless items. Anything to give them a burst of happy endorphins. I know the salary WOVE provided for Layla's security team was more than enough.

I turn back to Frank. "This will not end well for you."

He has a knife, and I can do nothing but watch as he lifts it up and brings it down on my thigh.

He fucking ripped my dress.

Yep. I will murder him.

I loved this dress.

Blood pours from the wound when he removes the knife, and I wait for my supernatural healing to kick into action... but it doesn't.

Fuck.

This human is using spells, which means a witch is definitely helping him.

"I can't wait to pluck those pretty little feathers of yours," Frank says. "Do you have any idea how much you're worth? The first known sphinx in hundreds of years!"

"Oh really? I hadn't noticed," I snarl.

He stabs me in the stomach.

Goddamn it.

I hope my mates hurry. I know they're on the way. I *sense* them. Can they feel my pain?

I feel their *fear*.

My head swims, my vision starting to fuzz around the edges from the blood loss. It's a strange experience as I've never had to worry about not healing.

But it's fine. My mates will save me.

Is this it? Is this why destiny brought them to me now? To save my life and kill this clan of hunters, essentially saving the lives of all their future victims?

Another human enters the room and whispers in my kidnapper's ear. His face scrunches in anger.

"I thought you said no one saw you steal the bird."

I scoff.

Rude.

I'm more lioness than bird.

"I had a cloaking spell," Erebos explains. "I made sure to send other guards away."

Frank shakes his head and turns toward the door.

"Watch her. We have company."

He leaves and Erebos leans against the wall across from me, arms crossed. In his human form, he appears as a svelte man, tall, with buzzed brown hair. The fucker smirks, letting me know he thinks he's won. He has no idea death awaits him.

I want to ask him more about why he needs the money. Why he turned on supernaturals to help *human* hunters. Griffins and sphinxes are so alike, basically cousins. Erebos turned on his *family.*

But then I realize I don't care. I don't need his explanation, and I don't want him to have a voice.

So, we stare at each other, me scowling and him smirking. We stay that way for at least five minutes before fighting erupts above us.

I must be in a basement.

It's fine. They'll still find me down here.

It's like my body is calling out to them with a pulse of energy. My heart aches as if being tugged towards them.

Gunshots ring out. Screaming echoes all the way down to our room. A small explosion shakes the floor.

"Are you getting scared yet?" I ask the griffin. He's put on a cool mask, but his heartbeat gives him away. His beady eyes keep jerking back and forth between me and the door.

It's the only way out. He can't escape.

He swallows hard and takes hold of his knife. His hand shakes as he holds the weapon up, ready to attack the first being that comes through the door.

He's got a knife.

I send the thought to Thorne who's just outside in the hallway. The griffin hears movement beyond the wall and leans close enough to put his ear against it.

Dumbass.

A gun goes off, sending chunks of the griffin's head my way. Thankfully, I'm back far enough that none gets on me.

You got him, I reassure Thorne and seconds later, a huge body barrels through the locked door, tearing it off its hinges.

Thorne rushes in with Layla right behind him. She runs to me as Thorne double checks that Erebos is dead.

"Seriously?" he growls, spotting the griffin. His human mask has dropped now that he's dead.

"He was greedy. The hunters paid him to help capture me," I say as Layla works to free me.

"If I had known, I would have kept him alive to torture him."

Layla finally gets the rope loose and it falls to the floor. I stand, then waver on my feet, needing to lean on Layla to avoid collapsing.

"The human stabbed me twice. I haven't healed."

"He must have suppressor salve on the blade," Thorne says, coming to my other side and wrapping his arm around my waist. "We should get you to a supernatural medic. They'll know what to do."

I mumble a response before my vision fades to black.

I wake up in Layla's king-sized bed with her sitting beside me, holding my hand.

"V," she whispers, her bottom lip quivering and tears streaming down her cheeks.

"How long was I out?"

"Two days. We were worried. You lost a lot of blood."

"What about the conference?"

"Postponed for at least two months."

I cover her hand with my paw.

"You saved me. You and Thorne. This was the reason."

I don't need to explain. She nods, knowing the reason these two were brought into my life now instead of decades or centuries ago was to save me in my weakest moment. It was only a matter of time before the hunters caught up to me.

"Did Erebos not realize that you two would have been able to find me?" I ask.

"I'm guessing he believed the spells placed on the room would have prevented the bond tracker from working," Thorne says, appearing in the doorway. He leans against the frame, arms crossed, looking so handsome in his black shirt and pants. "Normally, I can picture both of your locations in my head, but I couldn't see you this time. Whatever spell was placed on the room made it harder to picture you but it's as if our bodies knew where to go... as if following an invisible trail. It got stronger the closer we got to the abandoned building where they were keeping you."

"An abandoned building? How cliché. Where was this abandoned building?"

"Near JFK Airport in Queens."

Thorne walks into the room and joins us at the side of the bed. He palms my cheek.

"I heard your thoughts warning me about the knife. They were weak, but I heard them. You saved my life as well."

"Did you capture him? The human who caught me?" I ask.

Thorne winces. "He got away. There were at least a dozen humans in this hunter clan. We killed half of them."

"What I can't understand," I say, shaking my head, "is why they used wooden bullets in that first attack if they weren't targeting Layla."

"We managed to capture one human and get a little info from him before he broke the kill pill in his mouth. They wanted to kill Layla and incapacitate me so they could kidnap us both. Two for one deal. A gargoyle's horns and a sphinx's feathers. As for the second attack, Erebos planted the bomb in the SUV. The plan was to put Layla inside and pull you and me aside for whatever reason. Then the bomb was supposed to explode, killing Layla and causing a distraction and allowing the hunters to grab us. But when I stopped us just outside the door, sensing something was wrong, the hunters panicked, and they set off the bomb prematurely."

"Idiots," I grumble. "Is that all you found out?"

"Rory said they were also planning a bigger attack at the conference."

"Rory?" I ask.

"Yeah," Thorne chuckles, shaking his head. "Turns out I was right—he can read human minds. Some supernatural minds too, but they're not as easy."

I scoff. Rory is still creepy as fuck.

"Okay, if they were planning a bigger attack, then why the letter warning us to cancel it?"

"That's the confusing part." My mate shakes his head, clearly exhausted from dealing with this over the last few days. "My only explanation is that whoever put it there went rogue. There was never supposed to be a letter. Which is why we believe a witch is being forced to help the hunters. There are certain jewels that can be used to control witches, and whoever they have in their custody might have been trying to warn us."

Layla gasps. "I've heard about those jewels. That's absolutely horrible."

"It is." Thorne sighs. "I hate that I couldn't prevent this. I should have caught warning signs while vetting Erebos. He came highly recommended."

"Everyone has secrets," I say. "Even me."

"Oh yeah?" Layla laughs. "Do you plan on sharing them with us?"

I shrug and the vampire rolls her eyes.

Thorne places a gentle kiss on my lips, then turns to Layla.

"We should let her rest."

"I'm not tired," I say and yawn.

Dammit.

"You can barely keep your eyes open," Layla says, amused.

"Fine, but when I wake up, we're going to have so much sex."

"Oh, don't worry," Thorne says, giving me a wink, "I have an idea for that when you wake up."

Chapter 23 - Thorne

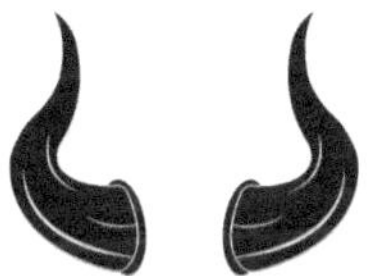

"**S**ky sex?"

Layla slowly backs up, inching toward the door of her penthouse. My wings are out as we stand on her balcony. It's the next day and Vara is fully healed. We have no obligations until tomorrow.

Tonight, we're fucking until the sun rises.

"No. I think I'm good," Layla says.

She turns, gearing up to run away from us, but Vara catches her by the throat.

With her mouth hovering over Layla's, she says, "Don't worry, Lollipop. You'll be so lost in orgasms that you won't even think about being high up in the sky."

Vara releases Layla and takes her hand, walking her to me. I wrap my arm around Layla's waist, and she tenses at my side.

"We've got you," I say, giving her a kiss on the top of her head. Then I catapult us into the air.

Layla screams and hooks her arm around my neck. She secures her legs around my torso and buries her face in my chest. Once we're high above the buildings and clouds, I stop and casually flap my wings to keep us airborne.

Vara joins us seconds later, coming up behind Layla.

"See, Bug? That wasn't so bad."

Layla lifts her head for a peek but doesn't loosen her hold on me.

Vara snakes her hands underneath Layla's shirt until she finds her breasts. She takes Layla's nipples between her fingers and pinches hard enough that she arches against me.

"All forgotten?" Vara asks.

"No," Layla moans and rubs her pussy over my stomach.

"So eager," I whisper and claim Layla's mouth.

While I have her distracted, Vara uses her claws to rip the crotch of Layla's leggings. She reaches for my pants next and fishes out my cock.

I moan into Layla's mouth as Vara fists my shaft, using my precum for lubrication. She kisses along Layla's neck and the vampire sighs against my lips.

"Such a good, brave girl," Vara purrs.

The sphinx guides my cock to Layla's entrance, rubbing the tip up and down the lips.

She's so wet for us.

"Thorne's going to fuck this pretty pussy now, okay, Bug?"

Layla moans and nods.

"And you're going to take my tail up your ass too," Vara continues.

I slide into Layla with one quick thrust, and she screams, her tight cunt still needing to stretch around me.

I stay seated inside and take hold of Vara's tail, waiting as she molds the tip into a solid form. It doesn't self-lubricate like mine, so I sink the tip inside her own wet pussy and make sure it's good and soaked before guiding it to Layla's asshole.

Layla's walls flutter around my cock the moment Vara pushes her tail in.

I start moving, fucking Layla while Vara's hand skims down Layla's front until reaching her clit though the torn fabric of the leggings. She presses down and massages.

"Fuck, yes," Layla moans. "I'm already close."

I pound her pussy harder and lean in, my fangs dropping.

Then, I bite her.

Bunny explodes with an orgasm, her walls massaging me.

When she's done shaking, Vara removes her tail, and I flip the vampire over my shoulder to the center of my back. She screams as I toss her around with ease and clutches my neck once she knows she's safe, and I have a secure hold on her.

"Hang on while I fuck Vara," I say and Layla's arm wraps around my neck so tightly, I'm almost unable to breathe.

I bring Vara into my arms, and she takes hold of my cock to guide the tip to her cunt. I thrust up into her, and she groans.

My tail finds Layla's pussy behind me, and it transforms to a phallic shape.

"I think Layla can take your tail too, Vara," I say.

I can't see it happening, but my body knows, shuddering with pleasure the moment Vara stuffs her tail inside Layla, next to mine.

This must be heaven. Fucking my two mates while between them.

Layla moans in my ear as our tails work in tandem, stretching her and pumping inside her. Vara whimpers in front of me. I kiss her to claim those wonderful noises and slide my hands over her ass, squeezing the soft mounds.

Layla gets brave and unlatches one arm from me so she can smooth her hand over one wing.

The sound I make is animalistic. Raw.

I'm about to lose it.

My mates' pleasure swirls within me, building to boiling point. My knot expands until I can no longer move it.

When someone's finger teases my asshole, I come.

My seed pours into Vara's pussy, and she kisses me fiercely. Our fangs clash. Blood spills into my mouth.

Vara moans, and her walls clamp down as she reaches orgasm next.

Between being double stuffed with our tails and the shared pleasure, it's too much for Layla to hold back, and she shakes with her second climax.

We remain mid-air, entwined like vines, for several minutes. I casually flap my wings to keep us high up. The night air cooling our heated bodies... well... except for Layla whose body is always cold.

"Okay," Layla begins. "I think I could get over my dislike of heights as long as we get to do that again."

I laugh and start flying us back down to Layla's balcony.

"Remove yourself from me, gargoyle. How many times do I have to tell you not to fly me when I have wings of my own?"

I shake my head. "I can't. One... my knot won't go down for a few more minutes. And two... I poured a lot of cum inside you. The knot is keeping it in. Can't have it slipping out and falling onto a human's head below."

She scoffs.

"That won't happen."

"It *has* happened before. It's why sky sex is frowned upon for winged creatures," I say, chuckling.

When I land, Layla dismounts my back, and she follows me inside the penthouse while I carry Vara. I smirk at her little huffs and whimpers as her pussy stretches and bounces around on my aching cock from the movement of my walking.

By the time we get to the massive bathroom, my knot has gone down enough that I'm able to lift Vara off and set her on the floor. Her eyes widen, and she looks down at her legs when my cum leaks down the inside of her thighs.

"See," I say and kiss her on the head. "Let's go clean you two up."

This was our last free night until the convention reconvenes in two months.

Vara and Layla will be busy with meetings and planning to reschedule appearances and panels. I'll also be busy working with Locheran on security since the hunters who kidnapped Vara are still out there.

I'm grateful we got to spend this time together, and I can only hope it's the first of many as our world shifts to a new reality.

One where humans and supes live together in peace.

But if it's war in our future, I will guard these two pieces of my soul with my life.

Epilogue - Layla
Two months later

Ever since Vara was kidnapped, King Xander, Locher-an, and Thorne have been focusing on finding the humans responsible. They believe it's a family, coming from a long line of hunters, who traveled to the city from Upstate New York after Erebos told them about Vara.

One of their hideouts in the city was found, but they must have been tipped off because it was empty when the gargoyles got there. They found remnants of ingredients used for spells, which further confirms they're using a witch to help them. Supernatural Crime Investigators are now looking into missing or kidnapped witch cases. There've been several over the last few years.

Tonight, a ball is being held to celebrate the final night of the rescheduled International Supernatural Conference.

My dress is a black bustier ball gown with a tulle skirt and sleeves that fall off my shoulders. The skirt is down to my feet, but thankfully, I'm wearing red stilettos so I don't trip over the fabric.

"My queen," Vara purrs, entering the room.

She's wearing a dress similar to the one she was kidnapped in. Apparently, the hunter ruined the original when he stabbed her, and it was one of Vara's favorite dresses. So she bought another one.

"My sphinxy poo."

"I'm leaving," she says, tossing up her hands and turning on her heel.

"Baaaabe." I snatch her hand and tug her back.

Vara can't hide her smile as she perches her arms on my shoulders while I place my hands on her hips. Her golden wings spread out and flicker with purrs of contentment.

"You love the silly nickname."

"I hate it, but I love *you*. I'll allow it, but I'll bitch about it the whole time."

"Deal."

"What are we making deals about?" Thorne asks, walking into the bedroom.

"That I can keep calling Vara sphinxy."

Thorne frowns. "What's my nickname? I never got one."

I smile mischievously, and he narrows his eyes at me.

"What about Flower or Rose Bud? Because roses have thorns?"

"Nevermind. I'm good."

I finally get a good look at him, and he's wearing a suit, all black of course. His long black hair is up in his typical man bun.

"Damn, BC, you're looking fine!" I say and giggle.

"BC?" He lifts a brow.

"Layla and I secretly call you that because you have a big cock," Vara says, her voice full of humor.

"Creative." Thorne sighs. "Let's go PIMA."

"PIMA?" I ask.

"Yeah. Pains in my ass."

He stalks out of the room, shaking his head, and Vara and I burst into laughter.

In the SUV to the venue, we cuddle in silence in the back seat. Until I can't take it anymore.

"I've been thinking... can gargoyles and sphinx have children?"

Vara sucks in a sharp breath, not expecting the question.

"I'm just wondering if that's something we'd want in our future. Kids, I mean. Vara, you said you're the last of your kind that you know of. What if you could have a little garga-sphinx baby."

"Pretty sure you just made up that word," she laughs.

"But could it happen?"

She sighs. "Anything is possible with supernaturals. Have I ever wanted kids? Not really. Was it expected of me? Yes. Then my species was wiped out, and I hadn't thought about it since. However, if there's a chance to save my kind... then, yes, I absolutely would have a garga-sphinx baby."

"I'd be honored to put a baby inside you," Thorne says, giving Vara a smile. Then he clutches my chin. "And you Layla. For all we know, our fated mate bond would allow *you* to have babies as well."

My heart beats excitedly at the thought.

The beats have become more frequent over the past two months. Not full-on pulsing, but it will flutter and come to life when something—or someone—excites me. To be fair, it's been dead for about 700 years. My heart has a lot of healing to do, and I think the bond, and my mates, is slowly reviving it.

But babies?

How would that even work for a vampire? Would the baby be undead? Would it be some feral beast with fangs?

My brain hurts thinking about the possibility of a vampire/gargoyle hybrid.

We enter the ballroom to find it packed with humans and supernaturals.

The unveiling plan has officially launched. Despite the conference being postponed, we received enough feedback from the community that they're ready to emerge from the shadows.

There's still a lot of work to do.

A PR plan being number one. We will set a reveal date, and a television broadcast will be made to announce our existence. Before that happens, we'd like to track down as many known hunters as possible and imprison them. The number of attacks on supes is still too high.

We find King Xander with his now wife Evangeline at his side. She's beautiful in her dark red gown with black designs sewn throughout. Beside Evangeline is a woman just as short and thick, but she has dirty blonde hair that's styled in waves around her shoulders. Her gown is dark blue, sleeveless, and fits her curves wonderfully.

Her name is Farrah, Evangeline's best friend. Before we can begin a conversation with them, Locheran walks up to our group, a scowl on his near flawless face. I rarely see the gargoyle with anything but a smirk or smile.

He does a double take when he spots Farrah. Apparently, Evangeline told her bestie about the existence of gargoyles... and other supes... a few weeks ago. She must still be adjusting because her eyes widen when spotting Locheran. He gives her a shy smile, which I find odd.

The gargoyle is anything but shy.

He shakes his head, his serious face returning.

"We managed to get surveillance images from a suspected safe house belonging to the hunter clan responsible for Vara's kidnapping."

He flips his phone around to show a large man with a head full of light hair, which I assume to be gray or blond since the image is black and white. He has a stubby nose and light eyes that must be blue.

Farrah gasps.

"What is it?" Evangeline asks, but her best friend shakes her head.

"I, um, just saw a human shift into a wolf."

Her face has paled more than usual. Her heart is racing in her chest.

I sense Farrah is lying.

Either she knows the man in the photo, or she's concerned about him killing off her new monster friends. Humans often lie so either one could be true.

I'll bring my concerns to Thorne and Locheran tomorrow. If I'm wrong, I don't want the night ruined. I'm not sensing malice from this woman. If anything, she's giving off defiance. Anger. *Betrayal*. Especially after seeing that photo.

"Send the image out. We'll talk strategy tomorrow," Xander says, slapping Locheran on the shoulder. "Relax tonight. Party. Find a beautiful being to fuck."

"Xander!" Evangeline scolds.

Farrah's pale face fills with color.

Oh. Okay. I get it now. This human has a crush on Locheran. I wonder if she fell for his charm and good looks while appearing human. It's hard to resist the gargoyle now in his true form.

Please don't ever tell Locheran that.

Thorne's jealous voice fills my head.

I turn away from our friends and place a palm on his chest, then Vara's, too, since she's standing next to him.

"Don't worry, my handsome protector, I only have eyes for two. Wait... that doesn't sound right. I have two eyes, but they belong to you two..." She sighs and rolls her eyes. "You know what I mean!"

"No, I have no idea what you mean," Vara says, goading me.

I roll my eyes and smile. "I was *trying* to say that I love you two."

"Good," Vara says. "Because I think I've loved you since you walked into my club almost two years ago."

Vara clasps her hand on my nape, pulling me in for a kiss.

When she releases me, I turn to Thorne.

"I want to hear it, BC."

He snarls at the dumb nickname. I admit it's dumb.

But it's still true.

"I think I've loved you since the first time you hid your smile from me. Now I get to see that joy every day. Because you, Queen Layla Sofia Aldana, are a bright day in my cloudy world and I bask in your ray of light."

Locheran gags behind us, and Thorne flips him off.

"It *was* a little cheesy," Vara says.

"Yeah, it was," Layla agrees. "But I'm a whore for cheesy lines. Feed them to me anytime."

I'm pretty sure Locheran mumbles gross before he walks away, leaving me with my mates.

My lovers.

My guardians.

They are so beautiful.

So beautifully *mine*.

The end

Thank You

Did you enjoy Guardians for the Vamp? Please consider leaving a review on Amazon, Goodreads, or StoryGraph. Or please share on your social media! Don't be afraid to slide into my DMs (as long as you're not mean)!

Want more monsters? Check out A Vow for the Vamp & Gaga for the Gargoyle if you haven't already. Locheran and Farrah's book, Giddy for the Gargoyle, is out now. Get it on Amazon! After their book will be Rory, the first vampire's book! You get more of his story in Giddy AND you meet the FMC!

Acknowledgements

Wow! Book 10! I can't believe it. I am having so much fun writing these monster books. I started writing characters in bigger bodies because I live in a bigger body myself. I might appear to have all the confidence in the world, but I don't. Everyday I hear people talking about going on diets, losing weight, hating that they've gained weight because lord forbid they get fat like me. It's exhausting so I wanted to make sure that readers in bigger bodies knew that their weight doesn't define them. That they're worthy of their love story. I also wanted to feature all body types in romance. Layla is more like a size 16, but I have characters that are size 20, 22, or mid-size. I might not get it right 100% but I'm trying and I will continue to write these types of characters.

Thank you to all my beta readers for helping me craft this story: Xan Garcia, Gina Hejtmanek, Mikaelynn Rose, Suzi Vee, Carlee Boscaino, Kascha Stern, and Kim Holsapple.

To my street team members: you are too good to me. Thank you for your support. I'm just a struggling indie author and you took a chance on me by helping spread the word about my stories.

Thank you to my editor Jenny Sliger with Owl Eyes Proofs & Edits. My comma defender! Thank you for letting me send you changes upon changes upon changes... and answering my Facebook messages.

To my cover artist: Ian. I am so in love with this cover. You plucked my characters directly from my head and turned them into these beautiful creatures.

And to the readers who have been with me from the beginning and to the ones who just found me, to the readers who buy my books no matter what I release, to the readers who constantly like my posts and share them... I love you all. You mean the world to me and you are the reason I keep writing!

Also by Settle Myer

Guardians for the Vamp

A Manhattan Monsters Romance

FFM with a Vampire/Sphinx/Gargoyle

The monsters of Manhattan are tired of living in the shadows. The new vampire queen, Layla, is tasked to come up with an unveiling plan, but she finds herself distracted by her new broody gargoyle guard... and the bossy sphinx on the unveiling committee. Find it on Amazon & KU.

Gaga for the Gargoyle

A Fated Mates Monster Romance.

Gaga for the Gargoyle is about 999-year-old gargoyle king, Xander, who has 6 months to find his fated mate before permanently turning to stone. Enter a strange dating app that pairs him with Evangeline, a 40-year-old human. This book is part of the Fated Dates series, a shared world about plus-size MCs meeting their monster mates through a mysterious dating app. Find it on Amazon & KU

A Vow for the Vamp

A Manhattan Monsters Romance.

500-year-old vampire queen, Millie, is ready to face the sun, no longer able to live with the guilt of the monster she's become. When she goes out for one last feed, she meets a 29-year-old golden retriever man named Teddy... who just might be the reason she lives. It's on Amazon & KU

Deadly Deceit & Deadly Obsession

Mafia Romance (New York City Syndicate Book 1 & 2) Deadly Deceit is the first book and Deadly Obsession is book 2. Both are standalones. They are dark cozy romance meaning the romance is sweet... but the story includes dark themes. Find them on Amazon & KU

The Off Script Series

Beyond the Bright Lights is the first book in the Off Script series of spicy standalone contemporary romances. It features Lana & Mylan's story. Beyond the Fame is book two and features Rebecca & Jensen's story. Beyond the Spotlight is the third and final book and features Savannah & Reynold's story. Find them on Amazon & KU. Beyond the Bright Lights & Beyond the Fame are on Audible

The Trinity Trilogy

If you love action & adventure, badass women with superpowers, diverse characters, found family, and fated mates—check out my sci-fi romance trilogy. Book 1 is a sweet romance with some cursing and violence, but books 2 & 3 have a sprinkle of spice in them. Trinity Found, Trinity Returns, Trinity Rises. Find them on Amazonand Audible.

About the Author

Settle Myer lives in New York City with her cats Zombie, Michonne & Birdie. She's currently a TV news writer who hopes to one day leave a world of death, disaster, and politics to write about worlds with plenty of cinnamon roll men and badass women. She loves all things zombies, cats, karaoke, and tattoos... but not necessarily in that order.

Social Media

Check out my website and sign up for my newsletter for updates on new books, discounts, and sneak peeks!

https://www.settlemyerauthor.com/

Join my readers group. Become a Settle Myer Star and be a part of the discussion with other fans. I also posts fun facts about my books, characters, and more!

Follow me on social media

tiktok.com/@settlemyerauthor

instagram.com/settlemyerauthor

facebook.com/settlemyerauthor

www.ingramcontent.com/pod-product-compliance
Lightning Source LLC
Chambersburg PA
CBHW021030310726
48969CB00006B/1603